A STABLE
WINNERS

EIGHT SHORT HORSERACING AND BETTING STORIES

BY RICHARD LAWS

First published 2022 by Five Furlongs

© Richard Laws 2022
ISBN 978-1-7397026-0-1 (Paperback)

Cover photography © Mr Michael Dunn

Contents

Duplicity

Despite the long car journey up the M1 from London, Joel Harvey was full of anticipation for his afternoon of racing at Thirsk, in North Yorkshire. Joel found he had a little spring in his step as he entered the racecourse. After all, it had all the makings of being a memorable day. He was set to interview one of the greatest jockeys of the modern era.

Using his journalist's press pass to access the course via the Owners and Trainers entrance, Joel was pleasantly surprised to find the course buzzing, even though the first race wasn't due off for another couple of hours. He'd been to Thirsk before, but many years ago, and remembered it as being a regional track with aging facilities desperately in need of rejuvenation. Like many of the smaller courses, the injection of cash from television rights had seen Thirsk able to invest and upgrade.

Joel walked into a premier enclosure that provided a fusion of old and new, and a feeling of regeneration. As he made his way around the parade ring, well-stocked borders and hanging baskets provided a feast of colour and scent. He passed punters discussing the day's sport, and others simply enjoying the clear, early-summers day. Imbued with a sense of belonging and anticipation, he stepped inside the brand new owners and trainers building and was greeted at the door.

The much vaunted, newly opened building for owners and trainers was a shade smaller than he was anticipating, but nonetheless impressive, and certainly a huge improvement on the crowded wooden hut he'd experienced on his previous visit. As was the case with most racecourses, visitors to the owner and trainers facilities were provided with large circular tables that accommodated up to twelve people, plus a self-service canteen. Table service was reserved for the Grade One courses. Upon trading a voucher provided as he entered the racecourse, a choice of sandwiches, or a hearty Yorkshire meal, were offered. He then looked to join a table wherever there was a space.

As a journalist, Joel was usually all in favour of this arrangement, as it meant he had the opportunity to sit down, uninvited, to lunch with all manner of people involved with the sport, not least the top trainers and owners, access to whom he depended upon for his living. However, today he was seeking a table out of the way, ideally entirely empty, so he could eat a light lunch and prepare himself to interview a jockey before racing started.

Despite the early hour, the room was surprisingly busy. Once he had his coffee, sandwich, and salad balanced on his wooden tray, Joel spotted an unoccupied table close to the windows overlooking the track. He made a beeline for it, settled himself in and started to eat his lunch.

No sooner than he'd taken his first bite and begun to chew, when an elderly gent sidled over to the table. Joel flicked his eyes up, but purposefully didn't make eye contact. He did notice the chap had a copy of 'Daily Racing News' under his arm, the paper that published his own weekly column. The man deposited himself a couple of seats away and with a contented sigh, unfolded and ruffled his paper, and began to inspect the runners and riders for the afternoon's meeting.

Joel groaned inside, he was almost certain this performance was a precursor to a conversation. Sure enough, the chap raised his bespeckled eyes over the top of his newspaper as Joel took his third mouthful of sandwich.

'Afternoon.'

Joel, still chewing a large mouthful of tuna bap, nodded over, initially unable to shape a response.

'Good afternoon,' he presently managed to get out with what he hoped was an apologetic overtone.

Still half hidden by his open newspaper, the chap didn't bother to look up, 'You'll be here to interview Lorrie, then,' he intoned in a heavy North Yorkshire accent.

When Joel didn't answer immediately, he folded the top corner of his paper down with a gnarly finger and inspected the subject of his question with inquiring eyes.

Joel swallowed the sip of coffee that he feared had burnt his lips, and carefully placing the cup back on its saucer, took a proper look at the fellow interrupting his lunch. His questioner was in his late fifties, not his seventies, as he'd first imagined. This judgement was based upon the receding, but not totally grey, slicked back hair and deep creases around a pair of intelligent blue eyes. On the thin side, but not worryingly so, the Yorkshireman had a round, weathered face that came to rest in a disarming smile, despite the presence of a whiplike scar that ran from his ear and around a few inches of his jawline. He was smaller than Joel, perhaps five-seven and wore a smart Harris Tweed three-piece suit, noticeably a shade too big for him.

'Yes, that's right,' Joel admitted pleasantly, 'I work for Racing Daily News. My name is Jo…'

'I know who you are, lad,' the chap cut in, folding his paper and placing it carefully onto the table, 'You're the young man who writes his column on a Thursday and does some of the feature interviews.'

'That's… worryingly correct,' Joel admitted with an automatic smile that soon vanished, 'You're certainly well informed, Mr…?'

'Aye well, it helps that they print a picture of you each time,' the chap said, tapping his finger on his paper and ignoring Joel's prompt to introduce himself, 'So you'll be hoping Lorrie rides his one-thousandth winner this afternoon?'

This was the sole reason his editor had been so keen for Joel to travel to a small regional racecourse for a Monday afternoon meeting of little note. High-flying star of the riding ranks, Lorrie Murphy, had a number of good rides today and was expected to reach the one-thousand winner mark, and in the all-time shortest number of rides. It was some achievement, and if he broke the record today, Joel's piece would be frontpage news in tomorrow's paper. He'd been delighted when his editor chose him; after all, he was only twenty-six and still a relative newcomer to the paper.

'It certainly looks like he'll reach a thousand today,' Joel replied levelly, beginning to tire of the chap's abrupt questioning technique.

'It'll only be a thousand if he gets *two winners* though,' Joel frowned, 'No, he only needs the one to reach…'

'Aye, that's according to the *official* numbers,' the old chap interjected knowingly, 'But he knows it's two. And he'll know why. You ask him - if you dare. I doubt he'll tell you.'

With that, the older man pushed himself up from his chair, placed a flat cap on his head and tucked his paper under his arm.

'Oh, and by the way, that feature you did on Freddie Cartwright last month was a sell-out. The man is an evil little swine and you painted him like he was some sort of god. Be careful not to get caught up in the mystique of these characters, my lad. Don't confuse the man with the success of his horses.'

He gave Joel a sullen nod and stalked off. Lost for a suitable retort, Joel watched the old man slip amongst a large group of owners milling around the entrance to the room. Alone at the table, he finished off half his sandwich and left his salad, no longer able to raise any interest in his food.

Joel stared at his plate, not really seeing it, his thoughts elsewhere. The rumour mill churned constantly within racing, and there were always people only too happy to knock a star like Lorrie off his pedestal with a salacious story. But to be fair, Lorrie rarely attracted that sort of attention.

His journey to the top rank of the sport had been quite different to most jockeys. Instead of burning bright as an apprentice for a season or two before working his way up the ranks, Lorrie's career had crept along under the radar for several seasons. A two-year period that consisted of a diminishing number of rides saw him move to Newmarket, and suddenly at the age of twenty-two his statistics began to reflect his talent. Initially he only rode for his base yard, seemingly preferring a quieter life, but then started to take race riding seriously in his mid-twenties. Joel believed Lorrie was a good example of how chasing rides, winners, and champion jockey titles wasn't the only way to succeed as a race rider. Lorrie Murphy selected his rides carefully and as a result had an incredible strike rate. Both owners and trainers spoke very highly of him, and to any seasoned race-watcher his ability as a race rider was undeniable.

The chap's comments rumbled through his mind. Thoughts of that interview and subsequent feature he'd submitted regarding trainer Freddie Cartwright caused a tightening in his stomach. The unnamed man had been right on the money, Cartwright had unsuccessfully tried to charm him, and as a result the trainer had revealed more of himself that he'd probably anticipated. Joel had written a piece that in the end, his editor had altered heavily. He'd had a gut feeling that Cartwright was disingenuous, and tried unsuccessfully to suggest as much in his writing, only to have it rejected. He'd re-written the piece several times and eventually the editor had stepped in and removed anything contentious.

'Joel Harvey?' inquired a bright voice nearby.

Lorrie Murphy was standing a few yards away looking incredibly fit, his Irish eyes sparkling. He wore jeans, t-shirt and an expectant grin.

Joel forgot the man in the Harris Tweed suit and went to work.

***

By twelve-forty-five, Joel had enough content for his interview feature. Lorrie had been a near perfect interviewee. The jockey came across as he'd expected; easy-going, intelligent, and accommodating. Joel could also see why owners were keen for Lorrie to ride their horses, as his answers were concise and insightful, qualities that would make him stand out among the race riding fraternity. The thirty-year old also possessed a self-deprecating sense of humour and a way about him that gave Joel the strong impression Murphy was driven, and honest. In short, Lorrie Murphy lived up to his public persona. That was, until Joel asked his final question.

'Racing fans are all hoping you'll achieve your one-thousandth winner, and with the rides you have lined up today, I expect you to be celebrating early in the afternoon,' Joel said, as he set up his question, 'Would you agree that you only need *one* winner to make it a thousand?'

Lorrie's eyes narrowed and he studied the reporter for a long moment.

Joel felt uncomfortable, but couldn't see the harm, 'It's just that… I spoke to someone earlier who seemed to think you were actually *two* winners away from that milestone.'

'Really? I don't know what you mean,' Lorrie replied distractedly, starting to get to his feet, 'I need to get going.'

'The chap was in his late fifties, and he had a scar on his… well, it went from about here…' said Joel, tracing an arc from under his ear and around the first two inches of his jaw and as he did, recognition registered on Lorrie's face.

Lorrie sighed heavily and bowing his head slightly, he surreptitiously cast his gaze around the room. The room was becoming busier, and a group of four people were approaching their table, eyeing the empty seats.

'Listen, I could just walk away, but I like your writing. I think you're someone who at least tries to write it as you see it. In truth, I phoned your editor and asked for you to interview me. I've spent the last twenty minutes deciding whether I can trust you, and I think I can. So, you're going to get a story about me that no-one else has heard.'

Joel blinked in astonishment. He wasn't expecting to be

on Lorrie Murphy's radar, never mind count him as someone who qualified as a regular reader of his column.

'Come on,' Lorrie said in a whisper, 'Let's find a quiet place to talk in private.'

Lorrie led Joel out of the Owners room, past the parade ring and up a few steps as if heading into the old grandstand. However, half-way up the turning steps, he went right and walked out onto a terrace whose aspect gave a perfect view of the track, specifically the view from behind the finishing post. The terrace was like a little lost corner, and completely empty. The two men walked to the end of the terrace and Joel joined Lorrie, leaning against the steel railings.

They both looked out and up the straight, taking in the view. Swallows were looping and diving over the track's pristine green turf, and on the inside of the course a great swathe of yellow shimmered as the flowering oilseed rape swayed in the breeze.

Joel waited. Good reporters didn't talk, they listened.

Presently, Lorrie swung his head around and the two men locked eyes.

'I've not told this story to anyone. Not even my wife,' Lorrie stated earnestly, 'But I guess it's time, now Jim is moaning about it again and the Guv's on the prowl.'

Joel looked perturbed.

'What's the matter?'

'Look, you've only just met me,' Joel muttered, 'Am I really the ideal person to be telling this story? After all, if it's as serious as you're making out, I might be forced to publish it, if it's a legitimately big story.'

Lorrie shook his head, 'No offence, Joel, you're in the right place at the right time. It's time to give up my story and besides, I've read your stuff. You'll make a fair job of it. I wouldn't be telling you if I thought you'd stab me in the back. Honestly, it will be a relief to share it with someone.'

'To be clear, what you're about to say is on the record?'

'Yes, unless you advise me not to continue.'

'And I'm to make the decision whether to publish?'

Lorrie grinned, 'Who else? I'm no writer. It's your call.'

Joel sucked in a deep breath and blinked his eyes wide, 'Okay then, fire away.'

'Good. Then I'd better start by telling you about the man at your lunch table. He is an ex-colleague of mine called Jim Wrigley. He was there when all this happened.'

Joel took out his notebook once again and began to jot down notes.

'You'll have heard of Patrick Greene?' Lorrie asked.

'Yeah, of course. That's where you started isn't it? You were with him for, what... three years?'

'Three years, four months.'

'I never got to meet him, but I'm told he was a real character and knew his job back to front.'

Lorrie nodded his approval, 'I walked into his yard in Malton when I was fresh out of school, a few months short of my seventeenth birthday. He put me to work with a brush and shovel. That's all I did all summer – shovel, brush, carry bales of hay and woodchip, and basically do all the jobs no one else wanted to do around the yard... he even had me creosoting barns, clearing out gutters, and fixing roofs. And you know something? I loved it.'

A half-smile of remembrance crept onto Lorrie's face, 'While I was carrying all that stuff around, working twelve to fourteen hours a day, I was getting fit. I walked in there as soft as clart. Within three months, Pat turned me into a human dynamo. A year later, when I turned eighteen, I was as fit as a butchers dog. That's when he taught me about horses and how to ride. Within another two months, I was riding out twice a day, as well as doing everything else he threw at me.'

The sparkle had returned to Lorrie's eyes, and Joel simply nodded to encourage him to continue.

'Pat was pretty old-school; he didn't think much to the young trainers who came along shouting about their analytical approach to equine care and training. He relied on his own experience and know-how of each racehorse.'

Lorrie slapped the top bar of the railings, 'You know, I was once ordered off a horse in the yard just before we were due to set off up the Wold gallop. I watched Pat run his hands down the gelding's spine and legs. The horse looked perfectly fit to me, yet Pat told me to go call the vet out. Sure enough, the gelding had a hairline fracture of his cannon bone... Pat had spotted it just by the way the gelding was pushing off his back foot. If I'd ridden him on the gallops, even just a swinging canter, that three-year-old might have broken down and maybe even lost his life. Instead, the horse recovered, was back racing the next season, and winning class four races for his owner.'

Lorrie paused, pursing his lips for a moment, 'I'm sorry, I'm getting too caught up with stuff that doesn't matter. The thing is, Pat was okay, *really* okay. He taught me a lot and treated me well. In return for my hard work he gave me a couple of rooms in a stable lads cottage, and it goes without saying that if it wasn't for him, I'd not be where I am now. So I don't want you to think I'm out to get him. I want you to make up your own mind. But I can tell you that Pat did like to get one over on the bookies and the racing authorities... and especially the racing authorities. Even as a young, inexperienced stable lad I knew he had no time for the people who ran racing.'

When Lorrie turned and slanted a nervous glance his way, Joel could sense a need for him to allay the jockey's fears.

'I could be waving goodbye to a really juicy story... but this conversation is now off the record. I'll only submit something to my editor if you agree first,' promised Joel.

'That's... very good of you,' Lorrie said with a grin, 'By the look of it, I've chosen an honest writer.'

This made Joel roll his eyes. He doubted any writer could claim to be completely honest.

Lorrie continued, 'Well, Pat Greene also bred a few thoroughbreds each year. I'd have been with him for about six months, but never had a ride in public, when I got a knock on my room door at about three o'clock in the morning in late January. It's Pat, and he says he needs some help with a mare in labour. It's freezing cold, there's ice all over the yard, and I'm only half-awake, but I pull my clothes on from the day before and drag myself down to the bottom of the yard. I'm a bit confused, as the Head Lad is just down the road in his cottage, and he's got bags of experience with these things, but Pat comes and gets me.'

'So, I walk into the birthing stable and Pat is on the floor, helping a foal come out hind legs first, which is never good news as it can pinch the umbilical cord, and he's screaming for me to check on the mare. Ten minutes later we've got a lovely filly. She's weak, the mare is stressed, and Pat is working on both of them, but I've not really done anything, so I'm wondering why it was so essential Pat called me out of bed. When I ask, 'Does he need me anymore,' he looks at me like I'm stupid and… well, five minutes later, I deliver my first ever foal and we've got another filly.'

'Twins?' Joel queried with wide eyes, 'I thought they were really rare.'

'Depends how you look at it,' Lorrie said with a shrug, 'Up to twenty percent of pregnancies in horses start off as twins, but both hardly ever get to be born. The risk to the mother is so great, almost all of the second foals are terminated after only a couple of weeks. It happens naturally to most, some breeders might help it along. It's much better for the mare to be safe and give birth to just one healthy foal. It's rare that twins survive, even rarer for them to be fit and strong.'

Lorrie fell silent for a long moment, looking out over the racecourse and to the fields beyond, as if contemplating this fact.

'I've a mind-bender for you,' said the jockey swinging around to face Joel, 'In the breeding of racehorses, it's a ten-thousand to one shot that twins are born and survive.'

'That's not great odds,' Joel admitted, 'So did the twins you helped to deliver survive?'

Lorrie grinned, 'After half an hour both the fillies were on their feet, trying to suckle. And I'm sitting there with Pat in the back of the stable with nothing more than the light of a single electric bulb, staring at these little wonders. And I tell him the foals look incredibly similar – and he agrees. He gets up and takes a closer look. Then he insists I do the same.'

'You know what the odds are for a mare to successfully deliver healthy identical twins?' asked Lorrie.

Joel shook his head.

'It's a hundred-thousand to one shot,' Lorrie said slowly, 'Pat pointed out that given the number of thoroughbreds born in the UK and Ireland each year, you'd have to wait more than fifteen years for the next set of identical twins to come along.'

'The two of us sat with our backs against the cold stone of the stable wall. It was the sort of cold that made our breath condense and hang in the air, mixing with the horses' breath to create a thick fog. Pat and I studied those two foals, not saying a word, transfixed by them. They were both bay fillies, with no distinguishing marks on their body, but they shared a thin, pearly white crescent that ran in a sweeping curve down their noses. When they stood alongside each other the effect was truly staggering.'

'Eventually the sun came up and it spurred Pat into action. He pulled me up with him and told me to go back to bed for a couple of hours, and most importantly, not to mention this to anyone.'

'These two are a very special gift,' he said, hardly able to take his eyes off the foals, 'And I need some time to work out what would be best for them, and the yard. So keep schtum, and I'll see to it you get a few rides in public.'

'I'm guessing he kept his word?' Joel asked.

'Oh, yes, and some. That summer he apprenticed me to the yard and I got the leg up on some of his best horses. I was nineteen and finished my first season as an apprentice jockey with twenty-one winners from only eighty-seven rides. I finished the 2004 turf season off by winning a valuable handicap at the York two-day October meeting. All but three of my wins that year came from horses stabled with Pat.'

'What happened to the twin sisters?'

'The day after the foals were born, the vet came into the yard and Pat took him to sort out the birth certificates and to microchip them. After that, he moved the mare and her foals to summer grass and to be honest, there was so much going on with me race riding two or three days a week, I forgot about them.'

Joel looked downcast, 'Oh, so that was it then... the twins never made it to the racetrack?'

Lorrie clapped his hands on the railings and snorted out a rueful laugh, 'Oh, yes, they made it to the racetrack alright. This is where your lunch buddy, Mr Jim Wrigley, comes into the story.'

Checking his watch, Lorrie began speaking again, but far more briskly than before, 'I've got twenty minutes before I need to get ready for my first race,' he told Joel, flicking his gaze to the ribbon of green turf that dwindled into the distance, 'Pin your ears back and you'll have my story in the bag before I go out there and try to deliver you a winning headline to your earlier interview.'

Lorrie began to speak, covering plenty of ground. Joel remained silent apart from a couple points of clarification. For a jockey who had hardly spoken a word to the press in the last six years, preferring to let his riding be his mouthpiece, Lorrie was incredibly articulate. The precision with which he described his story, recounting sights, experiences, and even smells, bordered on poetic in places.

Seventeen minutes later, Lorrie sucked in a lung-busting breath and breathed out slowly.

'How did I do?'

'You were phenomenal.'

'And the story?'

Joel blinked a few times, buying himself time so he could answer succinctly enough.

'It's… spellbinding. The audacity… his patience, and the execution…'

This prompted Lorrie's worried expression to melt away and flower into a broad grin, 'Good, I'm glad. Look, I've got to go, but I'll meet you back here after the second race. Yes?'

Content with Joel's promise and a handshake, Lorrie shot off to the weighing room. Joel watched him go with a smile playing on his lips, but once the jockey had disappeared from view he gripped the hand rails and stared down the last two furlongs of Thirsk's track, his mind in turmoil. How on earth could he ever do this story justice… and where would he publish it?

***

Lorries's Story
September 2006

Jim Wrigley was on the warpath. He'd already given a young stable lass a well-deserved dressing down that morning, and now he was marching across the compacted mud that served as the walkway to the paddocks, his jaw set, intent on taking the Guv'nor's golden-boy, Lorrie Murphy, down a peg or two.

He was going to enjoy this. The sly lad had been garnering the Guv'nor's favour ever since he arrived on his doorstep, scrawny, cold, just off the boat from Ireland. Winning a few races as an apprentice jockey was obviously going to the lad's head. It had been two years since the Guv'nor had taken Lorrie in, put a roof over his head, given him a job. And this is how the nineteen year old repaid him… by shirking his yard duties.

As Jim saw it, as Head Lad, he ran the yard and was the Guv'nor's right-hand man. It was his domain, and it was run to his own exacting standards. He'd joined the yard aged thirty-eight and been Patrick Greene's Head Lad for seven years. He was paid to crack the whip, to ensure the yard ran smoothly, and to keep the staff in line. Jim never lavished special treatment on any members of his staff – that wasn't the way you ran a racehorse stables, at least, not a successful one. And until now, the Guv'nor had been the same. But just lately there had been signs. Little moments where the Guv'nor had shown empathy for the Irish kid, and if there *was* any special treatment going around, Jim was going to make damn sure it stopped *with him*. Lorrie Murphy needed to be put in his place and told exactly how the land lay.

The numerous acres of paddocks were laid out like a chequerboard at the back of the racehorse barns with grass walkways between them. Even before Jim reached the first intersection, he was shouting.

'Murphy! Murphy, you shirker. Murphy!'

A small, waving figure emerged from a night shelter at the very bottom of the paddocks, where the homebred yearlings spent the summer months before entering training.

Lorrie waited patiently for Jim to stride purposefully, and with a certain pomposity, down the paddock walkway towards him. There was a knack to dealing with Jim, and Lorrie favoured the silent, deferential approach. So he stopped leaning languidly against the wooden shelter and awaited his superior by standing bolt upright and pasting a concerned frown onto his features.

Jim was good at his job and loyal to his boss, but in Lorrie's estimations, the forty-five year old spent too much time fussing over him. He'd initially feared the Head Lad. That had soon turned into a wary subservience. Once he realised his contribution to the yard was valued by the Guv'nor, he learned to cope with Jim's bombastic management style with muted respect mingled with pity. You worked hard for Jim, simply because it was easier than having him on your back all the time.

'What you doing way down here?' barked Jim from twenty yards away, throwing one arm in the air like an angry orchestra conductor.

Lorrie waited, sure there would be more. A moment later, Jim came to a halt within inches of his face and added, 'You were supposed to muck out the three stables before the horses finished on the walker. Two are still untouched and I've just put two horses into dirty stables.'

Lorrie picked up the tang of cigarette smoke on Jim's breath, mixed with the hum of body odour, the result of him riding out two lots earlier that morning. Jim never blinked his hard blue eyes and Lorrie was distracted by the small flecks of green around his pupils that he'd never noticed before. He began to shape a reply without really knowing where he was going.

'I was mucking out the…'

'I don't want to hear your excuses, boy. I want clean stables,' Jim cut in, his words heavy with condescension, 'So what brought you down here? Trying to hide away so you don't have to work?'

'*I instructed* Lorrie to meet me down here,' said the unmistakable East Yorkshire drawl of the Guv'nor, who placed great emphasis on the start of his sentence.

Lorrie raised an apologetic, and possibly amused eyebrow at Jim, who was still leering at him. The Head Lad immediately backed off a few yards, wiping a scowl from his face as Pat Greene stepped out from behind the night shelter.

'Sorry, Guv. I didn't see you there,' Jim blustered, 'I was… I didn't know you'd called for Murphy.'

'Yes, I heard,' Pat replied cordially.

Jim waited for an explanation, but when nothing else came from the Guv'nor apart from a withering stare, he was forced to shoot a conciliatory glance Lorrie's way.

His shoulders visibly drooped and thoroughly deflated,

Jim said, 'Right. Well. When you're finished here Murphy, those stables still need to be sorted out.'

Lorrie began to reply, but Jim wasn't listening. He'd already turned on his heel and was stumping back towards the main yard.

Pat had disappeared into the night shelter by the time Lorrie turned back, so he followed the Guv'nor into the small wooden shed that acted as a feeding bay and a place for the horses to take refuge from the worst of the weather.

'Here she is,' said Pat as Lorrie caught up with him. He indicated a filly by giving her a gentle pat on the side of her neck, 'What do you think?'

He recognised her immediately. The young filly was a decent size, albeit compact, and was already showing plenty of muscle. Lorrie felt she had the look of a juvenile sprinter about her. She bent her head into Lorrie's arm as he stroked her. With his forefinger, he traced the crescent of white blaze down her forehead.

'Is she the one I delivered over a year ago?'

Pat nodded, 'Yes, this is the one.'

'And you want me to take her on and ride her out?'

'All of that, and I also want you to ride her in her races,' Pat said with an amused smile.

'Why me?'

'Does there have to be a reason?'

Lorrie paused, 'Jim is going to give me a hard time over this. It would be good for both of us to be on the same page.'

Pat sighed, 'Jim is my problem, not yours. As for a reason, let's just say that I believe you have a future in racing. You're going to make a decent jockey, who in time could be great. But I also think you'll make an even better trainer. By seeing this horse through its entire racing life you'll learn more about racing than Jim, or even I, can teach you.'

Lorrie opened his mouth, then closed it again. Pat waited.

'What happened to the twin?' asked Lorrie.

'Died of colic a few months after I put her out here,' he said with a sniff, 'Crying bloody shame. I would have loved to race both of them together.'

Lorrie nodded and began to run his hands down the filly's legs, looking for unwanted heat, bumps, or grooves. Since Pat had taught him what to look for, it had become his automatic response upon entering any stable.

'She's already had a saddle on her back, and is very straightforward. She should be perfect as a little training project for you,' Pat added.

'Who owns her?'

'I do. And I won't be selling her, not even a leg. She'll run in my racing colours and under the yard's name. So what do you say, Lorrie?'

The nineteen-year-old grinned, unable to quell his excitement, 'I'm up for it, Guv'nor.'

April 2007

Lorrie had finished his morning shift and with the yard quiet, he dropped into the juvenile barn on his way back to his rooms in the cottage and cast his gaze down the line of inquisitive heads that popped out of their stables. He made for a box he knew well, and undid the latch.

'Luna!' he cooed at the bay filly with the thin crescent, producing a carrot for the young horse to munch on. He'd ridden her work for the last two months now, and although she wasn't going to be anything special on the track, he felt she had the ability to win a small race, probably a handicap, later in her two-year-old season.

After feeling her legs and back he gave her nose a rub and checked her manger water was free-flowing. He cleaned up the stable whilst the filly was still inside. She was a good-natured, easy to do sort, just as Pat had described her mother.

Lorrie had been talking and tending to the two-year-old

for almost half an hour by the time he slid the bolt home on her stable door, saying 'See you later, Luna'. As he set off for his rooms in the stable lads' cottage Lorrie reflected on his choice of stable name for the filly. He'd named her Luna, because of the creamy white, crescent shaped blaze down her forehead. He winced slightly as he walked down the barn, recalling the racing name Pat had decided upon.

'I'm calling Lorrie's filly La Duplicidad,' the Guv'nor had announced at the breakfast table that morning. All the stable lads and lasses had gone quiet.

'Why's that Guv?' Jim had asked.

'It's Spanish. As you know, my wife and I love it over there and it's the name of our favourite restaurant in Barcelona.'

'I can't even pronounce it,' Lorrie had complained afterwards to anyone who would listen to him.

He was half-way down the barn, trying to empty his mind of the horrible name the poor filly had been lumbered with, when a horse walked past the barn entrance thirty yards away. All the barns were open-ended to promote airflow, and a passing horse and rider wasn't uncommon, but it was mid-afternoon and the rider had looked unfamiliar. Picking up his pace, Lorrie jogged to the end of the barn and stared after the bay horse disappearing at a trot up the track that led to the gallops. He was sure it was the Guv'nor on top, and Pat hardly ever rode out. Besides which, you weren't supposed to use the shared gallops after one o'clock.

Summer 2007

At the start of May, Lorrie rode La Duplicidad in her first ever race at Redcar in a Maiden over five furlongs. There were ten runners from northern yards in the race and, despite being a shade slowly away, she stuck to her task admirably and finished in mid-division.

'She tries hard, has a decent galloping speed, but just lacks a change of gear,' Lorrie reported to Pat and his wife, Belinda, in the parade ring after the race.

Pat nodded his agreement and Belinda looked disinterested. They'd been married for fifteen years and Lorrie got the impression Belinda had expected life to be somewhat more luxurious. The realities of being a trainer's wife; long hours, a constant flow of people through your house, and the ever-present smell of horse manure, had worn away at her over the years. The days spent in the company of rich people drinking champagne at Ascot and Newmarket were too few and far between for Belinda's liking; an overcast afternoon at Redcar races being a poor substitute.

Now that it was clear the filly was set to be a handicapper, Pat lost no time ensuring Lorrie quickly ran the filly the three times required in order to qualify for a handicap mark. By the start of July, La Duplicidad was rated sixty-five after finishing fifth, and then seventh in two more sprint Maidens.

'There's a fillies-only sprint handicap for her at Thirsk at the end of the month,' Pat had mentioned to Lorrie the morning her opening handicap mark was published, 'We'll head for that and see how she gets on in a handicap. They'll go a slower pace in that sort of grade and it should mean she can save something for her finish.'

Lorrie prepared the filly by working her up the grass gallop on a Monday, four days before the race, watched by Pat. Afterwards, Pat announced he'd be away for a day or two to view a number of horses on behalf of a potential new owner, but he would meet him at Thirsk race on Friday afternoon.

'If everything goes well, we might be picking up a horse or two from a new owner later in the week,' Pat said in parting.

Friday morning arrived and Lorrie found himself alone in Wales, having slept overnight in the horsebox he'd driven there on short notice the evening before. Pat had called him on Thursday afternoon and asked him to pick up a newly acquired horse from a stud based near Chester. Upon his arrival in Wales, the stud owner had refused to allow the young horse to leave until he'd heard from the owner, so Lorrie had been forced to wait. The colt was duly released mid-morning on Friday and Pat instructed him to drive the horsebox straight to Thirsk for his ride on La Duplicidad. A stable lass would take Luna and his riding gear there, and the new horse would be fine housed in the racecourse stables for a few hours.

Lorrie arrived at Thirsk racecourse at one-thirty, only an hour ahead of his ride at half-past two. After sorting the colt out with a stable, plus feed and water, he rushed to the weighing room with minutes to spare, expecting to meet Pat for the first time in three days. When he walked into the parade ring, Pat was nowhere to be seen. Lorrie had a word with the stable lass leading up, but received an innocent shrug from the young girl.

'He said he had some business and disappeared from the racecourse stables half an hour ago. I had to tack her up on my own.'

It was only as the 'Jockeys, please mount' message came across the public address system that an unusually red-faced and nervous looking Pat caught up with him in order to give him a leg up into the saddle.

'She can win this, the opposition is poor,' Pat told him, checking the filly's breast girth.

Lorrie was about to reply, but something didn't feel right. The filly.. *his* filly didn't feel correct, there was something different about her… a little more bounce in her step, and the way she held her head was… wrong.

'Go round again,' Lorrie ordered the lass as they approached the chute, their exit onto the track.

Pat approached them at a trot, worry written in the furrows across his forehead, 'What you doing? What's wrong?'

'Something doesn't feel right, Guv'nor.'

The trainer glanced down at the filly, then slowly raised his head and locked eyes with his jockey. He considered Lorrie's confused stare and the lad's nervous body language – and took control of the situation.

'I'll take her from here,' Pat ordered the lass, and took the lead rein from her. As soon as she was out of earshot, Pat began to speak. He didn't look up at Lorrie, instead keeping his gaze set firmly on the narrow pathway running around the perimeter of the egg-shaped parade ring.

'You know?'

'Yes!' Lorrie hissed back from the saddle, 'This *isn't* Luna.'

'Keep your mouth shut and listen,' Pat growled angrily.

This was different. Lorrie hadn't heard this sort of raw belligerence from the Guv'nor before. He could be sharp, even angry every now and again, but never threatening.

'You'll ride this filly just like she was La Duplicidad. You'll get her out of the stalls, get her prominent and ride her into the lead over one furlong out and make sure you don't win by more than a length and a half, understood?'

Lorrie looked down onto the top of Pat's head and every ounce of respect he'd built up for the trainer over the last two years melted away. Pat kept his eyes on the pathway ahead.

'Okay,' Lorrie replied sullenly, physically overcome with numbness, but his mind on fire.

'You act happy when you come back in. You pose for the photos with a smile, and then you make sure you weigh in,' Pat continued.

'You don't speak with anyone about this horse, you don't do anything that could raise any sort of suspicion.'

Lorrie agreed once more and Pat led the horse into the forty yard long chute that would take them onto the racetrack.

'This is Luna's twin, isn't it,' Lorrie suggested quietly.

Pat didn't reply. He maintained his walk to the end of the chute.

'You're a cheat,' whispered Lorrie, 'And you've been stringing me along ever since that morning the twins were born.'

Pat stepped onto the racecourse and insisted on leading the filly right out onto the middle of the track before he made her stand. He stared up at his jockey, his intimidating eyes warning the young jockey of the consequences of failure. For the first time since he'd left his father, drunk, and screaming at him on the doorstep of his family home in Ulster at the age of sixteen, Lorrie felt truly frightened. The trainer grabbed his shiny black riding boot and squeezed it, his eyes popping in their sockets.

'Win this race, son. If you know what's good for you, win this race, and keep your mouth shut.'

Pat released his grip on Lorrie's foot, whipped the lead reign from the filly's bit and stood back, maintaining eye contact with her pilot.

As Lorrie gave the filly the command to jump off he called down, 'I'm not your son, Pat.'

The trainer stood motionless for a few seconds, watching the horse and jockey shrink inch by inch into the straight green arrow of turf bordered on both sides by shiny white running rails. Presently he drew in a deep breath and grimly strode off the track and towards the grandstand.

***

Joel was jolted back from his thoughts of Lorrie's past experiences by the public address system declaring in a suitably loud and strident voice the second race was off. He'd been so lost in Lorrie's story, he hadn't noticed the viewing position he'd previously shared with the jockey was now thronged with race-goers, all looking up the track to their left as the runners in a Novice event raced towards them over the straight five furlongs.

Lorrie was riding the third favourite in the betting. His expected one-thousandth winner was later on the card, an odds-on shot for his Newmarket trainer in the feature race of the day. Joel began watching the race on the huge screen in the centre of the course.

Tucking his mount in behind runners, Lorrie's trademark stance in the saddle was soon in evidence. Much had been made of his ability to keep a horse balanced, remain calm, and transmit confidence into the horses he rode, thus enabling a horse to conserve energy in the early stages of any race. A combination of tactical awareness and patience then took over as the race began in earnest. Lorrie waited for a gap to appear, and over a furlong and a half out he urged the colt forward under hands and heels encouragement.

At the furlong pole he gave his mount the tiniest of touches with his whip, flicking it, rather than slapping the young horse, and the colt proved a willing partner, striking for home and swiftly putting the win beyond doubt.

Up in the Owners stand, Joel grinned. The grin soon faded though as a new thought struck him. He found himself wondering whether Lorrie had just staged a replay of his winning ride on La Duplicidad from twelve years ago. It was remarkably similar to the description of how he had won the race on the wrong racehorse, on the same track, all those years ago.

A cheer rose from the small, but knowledgeable Yorkshire race-goers and a round of applause broke out even before the race caller reminded the crowd that Lorrie Murphy had just ridden the one-thousandth winner of his riding career.

Joel joined the river of people flowing down to the parade ring, and massed with them around the winners' enclosure. Lorrie smiled appreciatively to the happy throng as he received their appreciation with innate modesty and a strangely endearing embarrassment. He shook hands, smiled for photos, and signed race-cards before disappearing into the weighing room for that all-important rubber stamp from the Clerk of the Scales, that would make the one-thousandth win of his career official.

'I thought about refusing to weigh in. I got into the winners enclosure and Pat was all smiles, and I seriously thought about just walking out of the course in my silks,' Lorrie had told Joel before he'd left to get ready for his first race.

'But I was young, scared, and really worried I'd ruined my entire racing career, so I did as I was told. I plastered a smile onto my face and weighed in. Once I'd accepted a bottle of champagne for the win, I went out to the back of the weighing room toilets and threw up, even though I'd hardly eaten anything.'

As Joel studied a smiling Lorrie emerging from the weighing room after a quick change of clothes, he doubted that today would see a repeat of that particular episode in Lorrie's story. That said, the day wasn't over.

Lorrie signed a few more race-cards, thanked another tranche of well-wishers, and even conducted a short interview with a TV crew on his way over to where Joel was standing outside the winners' enclosure.

'Thanks. Come on, I've got an hour before I ride in the four o'clock,' he said, accepting Joel's congratulations but displaying a keenness for concluding their interview. He grabbed Joel's arm and guided him towards the winning connections' lounge.

'The owners aren't here, so the Clerk has offered me this winning connections' room for the next thirty minutes,' he explained, 'That's just as well. I've only got about twenty minutes before I need to get changed for the feature race.'

Joel was guided into a small room a few doors down from the weighing room. It was filled with sofas, a large television, and a beaming lady behind a tall, thin counter. She immediately offered them both a drink, suggesting a glass of champagne with an enticing smile. Having served them two orange juices, she gave them both another glowing smile and promptly left the room, closing the double doors firmly behind her.

Lorrie was clearly keen to get on and finish relating his story, and Joel wasn't about to delay him. They took a seat at each end of a sofa and Joel picked up from where he'd left off.

'I only had the one ride that day in 2007, so after I got changed I went to find Pat. I wanted to quit, tell him how disgusted I was with him. But he'd gone, leaving the stable lass to sort out La Duplicidad on her own. Pat had told her I'd drive both horses back home. I did so in such a foul mood. It was probably a good thing that neither Pat or his wife were there when I arrived; I was ready to lay into him for the way he'd manipulated me.'

'I suppose you felt hurt, let down by someone you trusted,' suggested Joel, 'And I imagine he'd profited from the filly's win as well.'

Lorrie had been sitting on the edge of his seat, but now he leaned back and sighed, a disconcerted look on his face.

'You know something, I don't know why, but at that moment I was so focused on how Pat had played with me, and having… broken the rules of racing, I hadn't even considered his real motivation. I've tried to analyse why I went through with the deception, and come to the conclusion that I still wanted to believe in Pat. Maybe that's why I went ahead and won the race for him, because deep down, there was still a piece of me that couldn't come to terms with the glaring truth; that Pat Greene was a crooked trainer.

'When you left to ride in the last race I took the opportunity to view the video archive of that race. You won it doing cartwheels, but I reckon you didn't have to try too hard,' Joel commented carefully, not wishing to upset the jockey.

Lorrie stared gloomily out of the window and onto the

lawn in front of the parade ring, 'I could have won it by fifteen lengths if I'd wanted. But I didn't. Like a good little boy, I won it by a length and a half, just like Pat told me to, making it look like I was actively riding the filly out. It makes me sick to my core even to think about it. I've watched the replay a few times and it feels like I'm reviewing an amateur dramatics production with me hamming it up as the lead.'

Sensing he needed to move the conversation in a new direction, Joel asked, 'So what happened when Pat got back to the yard on the night of the race?'

'Before he arrived, I needed to confirm Luna was okay, but of course she wasn't in her usual stable. Pat must have taken her to wherever he'd been stabling her twin. I stomped around the yard, looking everywhere. Funny what you find when you're searching for something quite specific. I found at least three horses squirrelled away in outbuildings and quiet paddocks, but no Luna. Then I remembered he sometimes leased a few fields from another trainer.'

Lorrie smiled warmly, 'I found her down in a little valley about a mile away from the yard. It was a pain to get to, but I reckoned Pat could have trained Luna's sister from there at a push. She was sharing the field with a couple of older horses who were out there recovering from injury.'

'When I got back to the yard it was starting to get dark, and once in the heart of the stables, I could see lights on in the main house. As I walked closer, I could hear the sound of Pat's wife, Belinda, laughing. The door to the kitchen was always open, so without much preparation, I let myself in and burst into their lounge to find Pat and his wife drinking champagne, the re-run of the race playing on their television. I was all set to scream blue murder at him, but was distracted. Pat grinned, whilst his wife just smirked, and behind them, on their dining table was a mountain of money. It was stacked feet high and wide.'

'You know something,' said Lorrie in a faraway voice, still lost in the image, 'I'd still not considered he was betting on the race. It seems so stupid of me now, but back then, I didn't think that way. I was caught up in how he'd cornered me into cheating for him. Until that moment I hadn't considered he could have any motive, other than being desperate to win a few races with his horse, and in doing so, also chalk up a victory over the racing authorities.'

A thoughtful silence descended on the winning connections' room and Joel thought about asking another question, but decided against it. Lorrie adopted a mournful, glazed expression for a long moment, but soon shook himself and checked his phone, declaring he had to leave for the next race in a few minutes.

'One minute,' he said, holding an index finger up at Joel. He made a call that was picked up immediately, and after only a few words that meant nothing to Joel, Lorrie told him, 'I'm going to leave the story to be finished by someone else, someone better placed to give you everything you need.'

Joel's frown turned to incredulity when Jim Wrigley pulled the door of the room open, stepped inside, and was greeted by a grinning Lorrie who shook the older man's hand warmly.

'My apologies for my behaviour at the table in the owners and trainers lounge earlier,' Jim said with a twinkle in his eye as he took Lorrie's place on the sofa, 'Lorrie was keen, but I wanted to meet you before we made the final decision.'

'The final decision?' Joel queried, happy to forget his new interviewee's mild deception earlier in the day.

'The choice of writer to tell our story.'

'Ah...' Lorrie said in a sheepish tone. He was standing by the door, cringing slightly, 'I hadn't quite got around to...'

'Don't worry, I'll explain,' interrupted Jim waving a couple of fingers at the jockey as if to shoo him out of the room, 'You get ready for your next ride.'

Lorrie grinned and departed without another word.

Jim rolled his eyes at Joel and gave a little shake of his head, 'He still needs me around to clear up his mess.'

29

'It appears you are good friends,' stated Joel.

Jim gave him a half-smile, 'Yes, but it wasn't always that way… so where'd he get up to?'

Joel consulted his notes, 'Erm… he'd gone into Pat Greene's house and found a large amount of money stacked up on the dining table.'

September 2007
Jim Wrigley's Story

This was the day Jim had been waiting for with grim anticipation. Young Lorrie was a good rider, a nice, honest lad with plenty of potential, but he was also terribly inexperienced in life. He had no clue how corrupting a sport built around gambling could be, and in Jim's view the boy was woeful when it came to judging people. He'd tried to take him under his wing, but the Guv'nor had already filled the lad's head with his manipulative bile. All Jim could do was watch and wait.

The Guv'nor insisting he took a day off when the yard had a runner had got the warning bells ringing in Jim's head. He was always on hand when there were runners to prepare and get off to the races, that sort of menial work was beneath the boss. When that runner was the horse the Guv'nor had gifted to Lorrie, in his words, 'for the boy to train', then Jim knew some sort of plan was afoot. Pat Greene wasn't interested in anyone other than himself. Upon learning Lorrie had been sent to Wales the day before the run on some unimportant errand, and Pat was nowhere to be found, Jim knew for certain that things were coming to a head.

You might ask yourself why a Head Lad like Jim, with twenty-five years' experience, would stay in such a role. It's the same reason he knew the Guv'nor was up to something – Jim had been caught out by the trainer five years earlier. If he left the yard, Pat Greene would ensure Jim never worked in racing again.

During the day, Jim watched the odds of La Duplicidad fall from forty to one in the morning to around fives before the race, and feared the worst. He'd decided there was nothing he could do… pitching up at Thirsk would be of little value, as he was sure Pat would still be exerting his influence over the boy. Besides, he wasn't too sure Lorrie would trust him; Pat had been grooming the young lad for over two years. He had to let things play out and hopefully pick up the pieces once the race had run.

The Guv'nor was staging a betting coup. He'd done so twice before to Jim's knowledge, and Pat Greene favoured an insidious method of operation. He would involve impressionable youngsters to do his dirty work, usually without them realising what they were getting themselves into, until it was too late. By that stage they'd be in too deep and while the Guv'nor would be a step or two away from any wrongdoing, the youngster would be implicated, and that's when Pat Greene would turn the screw.

History was repeating itself, and Jim expected there would be collateral damage – there always had been in the past. Although this time, Jim couldn't understand how on earth the filly would improve enough to warrant such a plunge on her. However, Jim was sure this would become apparent soon enough.

He didn't back La Duplicidad. He felt doing so would only tar him with an already dirty brush. Jim watched the filly win and late in the afternoon made his way back to the yard, secreting himself on the roof of one of the older stables that overlooked the main yard. There he lay for a couple of hours, waiting for the return of the Guv'nor.

Lorrie arrived back at the yard first, so Jim slid down a drainpipe and keeping at a safe distance, watched him for any clue as to what was going on. Jim assumed the Guv'nor had tricked him, and he'd not got the lad completely wrong… As he watched the lad lead the horses into the barns, Jim hoped with all his heart that Lorrie wasn't in on the deception.

Whatever con the Guv'nor had come up with, he would want to replicate it if he could. If the boy's career wasn't already ruined, it would be soon enough, which wasn't right, as Jim was of the opinion that Lorrie had huge potential as a jockey and a horseman.

Jim knew every horse in the yard intimately, even the boy's Luna. In order to elicit such improvement in the filly, Pat Greene must have done something serious, and Jim feared the matter might still be picked up by the racing authority's drug testing regime.

With the new horse from Chester and La Duplicidad both settled into their stables for the evening, Jim expected the lad to make his way back to the stable lads' accommodation. Instead, he followed at a distance as Lorrie spent over an hour scouring every barn, stable, pen and paddock… for something. He was sure the boy was becoming more agitated with every moment that passed. Eventually he tracked him out of the yard and into the Wolds, and a large paddock in the bottom of a valley. He watched as Lorrie crossed the huge field to approach a horse that looked a lot like… and in a flash, Jim knew how Pat Greene had masterminded the coup.

Lorrie had set off back to the stables at a run. Jim hurried after the lad, trying to catch him before he reached the yard, wanting to calm him, advise him… stop him making the same mistake he himself had made five years ago. But by the time he reached the stables, the lad was nowhere to be found. However, there was a light on at the Guv'nor's house and if he wasn't mistaken, he could hear the lad shouting.

Throwing caution to the wind, Jim sprinted across the large quad that marked the centre of the yard and headed for the Guv'nor's house. It was set back from the quad, perfectly located to face the line of stables and entrances to the three main barns. Anyone looking out of any front-facing windows would have spotted Jim straight away. Ignoring this danger, he hurdled the waist-high privet hedge, crossed a lawn and small rockery, and sidled up to a lounge window that was slightly ajar. Crouching below, his back scraping the seventies stippled red brick, Jim tried to steady his breathing as the argument between Pat and Lorrie built in volume.

'I've found Luna,' Lorrie said coldly.

'So what?' said a woman's voice that Jim recognised as Belinda, Pat's wife.

'You switched her with the identical sister!' Lorrie spat.

Belinda giggled. She sounded slightly drunk.

'Come on, Lorrie. No hard feelings,' Pat said smoothly, cutting across his wife's condescension, 'To survive as a trainer you have to bend the rules a little and take a profit when you can.'

'You knew what you were going to do with those twin sisters right from the start, didn't you?'

There was a pause. Jim heard a smacking of lips and imagined Pat had just drained his glass of whatever he was drinking.

Presently, Pat replied, 'Of course, stupid boy. Do you think I'd pass up an opportunity like that? Identical twins are so rare no-one would ever imagine…'

'What about the microchips and passports?' demanded Lorrie.

'Oh dear, you really are unimaginative,' commented Belinda in the background, 'You get the first one chipped, then invite the vet back a week later and tell him it's not worked. He checks, says 'Never mind,' and sticks another replica chip in the horse's neck… only it's not the same…'

'Alright, my love, enough,' Pat said sharply, silencing his wife.

There was the sound of a heavy glass being placed on a wooden surface, 'So you're here for your cut?' Pat queried, a slightly amused note in his voice.

Jim fought the urge to jump up and scream, 'No!' through the window. Instead he froze, his eyes slammed tightly shut, praying the boy would make the right decision. This was how Pat operated. He would force you to mistakenly do his evil work, then reward you, drawing you further into his web of deceit. Jim knew this. He had first-hand experience.

'What's the harm, Lorrie? You've earned it,' Pat assured him, 'No one will know you've benefitted...'

There was the thump of something being dropped, along with the faint riffle of paper. Jim could see himself, five years previously, watching Pat slap wad after wad of money down on his work desk, as he bought off his Head Lad...

Jim was torn from the scene of his past by Lorrie's reply. The boy was angry. He was broadcasting his words with such viciousness, Jim didn't know whether to cheer or rush into the room to stem the violence that must surely follow.

'You're a cheat. Keep your dirty money,' accused Lorrie. He sounded emotional, his voice shaky.

'I may be a cheat, but so are you.'

Pat's response was delivered in a cool, matter of fact manner and it silenced Lorrie.

'You rode a horse, *your* horse that *you* have trained. You also knew it wasn't the horse declared for that race. You didn't report it. And, you placed bets on that horse...'

'No I did not!'

Ah, but you *did*,' Pat said with mock sorrow, 'Every online bookmakers account I set up to back La Duplicidad I put in the name of Mr L Murphy. You really should store your drivers' licence and passport in a safer place than the top drawer of your bedside cabinet. And of course, I know your bank details because I pay you every month. Now, if someone were to tip off the racing authorities I think you'll find I'd be exonerated and you... well, you can guess the rest.'

Lorrie, his anger making his voice sound harsh and rasping, bellowed a torrent of abuse at the trainer. Once it had started to lose its initial fire, Lorrie screamed, 'I quit. I'm out of here tonight!'

'Oh, I don't think so,' countered Pat levelly. This prompted another giggle from Belinda in the background.

'You haven't finished yet. This scam is perfect, and I haven't spent two years getting it all set up for you to ruin my plans by disappearing!' Pat exclaimed, 'We can run this for years... waiting until your filly falls back down to the right handicap mark and then sending out her twin to mop up.'

'And if you do try to leave, I'll see to it that you never work in racing again. Think about that before you pack your bags, Lorrie.'

There was the sound of footsteps inside the house and a door slammed. Jim left his position under the window sill to the sound of Pat and his wife laughing and quaffing champagne.

He tracked Lorrie down to his stable lads' cottage, finding the lad's bedroom door ajar. When he tentatively pushed it open, Jim discovered Lorrie red-faced, tear-streaked, and still extremely angry. Clothes were strewn around the room, but not packed.

'Oh great,' the boy said bitterly, 'That's all I need. He's sent you to make sure I don't leave, eh?'

'On the contrary,' Jim replied quietly, closing the door and clearing a space on the bed in order to sit down, 'I'm here to help.'

Lorrie rolled his eyes defiantly, 'Brilliant. That's all I need. Help from Pat Greene's right-hand man. I bet you knew all about his masterplan to ruin my life!'

'Just listen,' Jim insisted.

Jim talked in a low, meaningful tone for half an hour and Lorrie did as he was told, and listened.

***

July 2007
Catterick Racecourse

Jim checked the time: two-fifty-five in the afternoon.

He'd been following Pat and Belinda around the track for two hours. La Duplicidad was due to race in five minutes and the trainer was leaning against the rails close to the parade ring chute, watching the sister of the filly go to post with apprentice jockey Lorrie Murphy aboard.

Making sure he wasn't seen until the last moment, Jim approached the trainer and his wife from behind. He need not have worried, both of them were too busy tapping at their mobile phones to notice him in their peripheral vision.

'Afternoon, Pat. Checking the latest prices of La Duplicidad. I see she's been backed from twenty-five-to-one down to seven-to-two second favourite,' said Jim.

Pat looked up and frowned, 'What you doing here? Who's looking after the yard?'

Jim ignored him, 'What size stake have you got riding on the twin's sister today?'

Belinda began to say something about Jim minding his own business, but Pat immediately silenced her, realising something was wrong.

'Why are you here?'

'To ensure the correct result of course.'

Pat licked his bottom lip nervously, 'What do you mean?'

'The boy,' Jim replied, nodding his head towards the five furlongs start in the distance, 'He's going to throw the race. Lose on purpose, just to get back at you. I heard him talking to one of the other lads as they came back from the gallops the other day.'

Jim now had their full attention. He continued, 'I can make sure he doesn't lose.'

'He's talking rubbish,' Belinda scoffed, taking her husband's arm and pulling at it in order to turn away. Pat studied Jim and a cold shiver ran through him. His Head Lad was controlled, confident, and had a steely look in his eye that hadn't been there for many years. This was a serious development.

'Leave,' Pat told Belinda coldly, shaking his arm from her grip, 'Jim and I need to talk.'

Belinda huffily crossed her arms and glared at her husband for a moment. She received an ice-cold stare in return and with a dissatisfied snort turned on her heel and flounced away.

'One phone call will make sure he doesn't lose,' Jim said, brandishing his mobile phone meaningfully, 'And your money will be safe. All I need you to do is read this, and I'll record it on this audio recording app I have on my phone.'

He handed the trainer a single sheet of paper with half a dozen typewritten lines in a large, easily readable font. Pat inspected it and gave a derisive snort of his own.

'There's no way I'm going to read this out aloud.'

The public address system burst into life from the grandstand, announcing the fact that the horses for the three o'clock race had gone behind the stalls.'

'Fine,' Jim said with a shrug, 'He'll throw the race, and you now have less than a minute to lay-off the tens of thousands of pounds you've carefully invested with dozens of bookmakers on and offline. Face it, you know the boy's on a short fuse. Haven't you noticed he's been getting more and more flakey in the last few days? I think he's close to a breakdown. This is the last time you can use him, and he's likely to cause merry hell for you and the yard when he tells everyone after the race. But I can make all of that go away.'

The blood drained from Pat's face. He glanced up the track and gulped in a large breath.

'How will you make sure?'

'He won't lose. Now, read the statement.'

The public address system crackled back into life and the crowd were informed that the loading process had started and the heavily backed La Duplicidad was one of the first of the fourteen runners to load.

Jim held his phone up and Pat began to speak quickly and, in parts, through gritted teeth, 'I, Patrick Greene, being of sound mind, on the fourteenth of July 2007, do solemnly declare that I, and I alone, was responsible for the coercing of Mr Jim Wrigley and Mr Laurence Murphy in the matters of…'

Once he'd completed the thirty-second speech, Jim tapped the screen of his mobile and checked the recording length, swiftly shared the audio file with two email addresses then sent a single, pre-written text message.

At the five furlong start, a stalls handler Jim had once shared digs with as young work riders, checked his pocket when a text alert sounded, then went over to the horse in stall three and called something to the jockey.

Lorrie's heart was thumping, not with nervousness for the race, but with relief.

'Three to go!' shouted the starter.

Lorrie slid a hand down to his boot, then underneath to where the breast girth lay up against the horse's chest. He located a small tab and pulled at it. There was a quiet ripping sound and his saddle immediately slipped to the right.

'Sir! SIR!' he screamed, climbing into the frame of the stalls to wave at the Starter before resuming his partnership with the filly.

On the Starter's command, four stalls handers converged on stall three, opening the back gate. La Duplicidad backed out of his stall and Lorrie immediately slid off her back and shook his head mournfully at the Starter, indicating the torn saddle straps, now hanging from the filly's back.

The starter nodded, a shout of 'Jockeys!' went up, the stalls clanged open and thirteen thoroughbreds kicked forward to the sound of encouragement from their pilots. Behind the stalls Lorrie led his filly away, feeling like a huge weight had been lifted from him.

'And they're away,' called the commentator in the stands, 'And they've gone without the heavily backed, La Duplicidad whose tack seems to have failed.'

Pat Greene rounded on Jim, his face contorted into a trembling mask of barely contained fury. All around them, race-goers had massed to watch the race and the race commentary provided a wall of constant sound. Pat opened his mouth but seemed unable to exert enough control over his vocal chords to vocalise the extent of his discontent. Yes, as a non-runner his stakes would be returned, but this was about a lost opportunity. He'd bet big this time, big money, late in the day, knowing this would be the last run for La Duplicidad – Lorrie Murphy had been falling to pieces in the last month, he'd become an unhinged, glassy-eyed wreck. The pressure had got to him… And then, the penny dropped. It had been an act, a ruse to paint him into a corner, a corner so tight he would make a snap decision…

As Pat continued to glare at him in mute rage, Jim tried hard not to flash his ex-boss a self-satisfied smirk, but failed.

'I promised I'd make sure you *didn't lose*, Guv'nor. I didn't say anything about making sure you'd win.'

***

Joel reclined into the sofa and whistled softly.

'Weren't the two of you taking a big gamble that Pat would fold and accept your conditions?' he asked.

'Not really,' Jim shrugged, 'Pat Greene had become obsessed. That small race at Catterick was to be his grandest, greatest touch, and we were careful to give him only seconds to decide between success or failure.'

He looked thoughtful for a moment.

'I have to say though, Lorrie's idea to pretend to be slowly going insane with worry and the strain of riding a cheating horse over the three months between the two races was a masterful touch.'

Jim nodded towards Joel's notebook.

'You got all that then?'

'I think so…'

'Come on then,' he said, standing up, 'There's more to

come. You're going to be busy if things work out the way I think they will.'

Joel followed the older man out of the winning connections room and across the paddock lawns into the grandstand enclosure. He took up a position on a small paved hillock and peered down the track to where the runners for the feature race were entering the stalls.

'This is Lorrie's last ride today,' Jim stated, 'It seems fitting that it's over the five furlongs at Thirsk.'

Joel started to correct him. Lorrie had another two rides in later races, surely Jim had forgotten. However, the race commentary burst into life at that moment, drowning out his words.

Lorrie's mount jumped from the stalls well, and as an odds-on shot should, pulled clear of his rivals just over a furlong out, under a positive ride. Hailing from the southern yard he was now attached to, Lorrie allowed the four-year-old gelding to coast home in the last few strides and record a length and a half victory. The Yorkshire crowd showed its appreciation with a round of applause and a hum of contentment. Favourite backers up and down the country marked off another Lorrie Murphy win and queued up for their winnings.

'Come on, let's see the presentations,' suggested Jim as they watched the first three horses home enter the chute to the winners' enclosure. He immediately darted off, leaving Joel to catch him up and marvel at the extraordinary energy the Head Lad still possessed at the age of sixty.

As he entered the semi-circular winners enclosure directly outside the weighing room, Lorrie tipped the brim of his cap to acknowledge another round of applause from the crowd. He slipped off with the minimum of fuss and spoke to the trainer and connections then disappeared inside the weighing room. Emerging two minutes later, still wearing the winning silks, he accepted a small trophy for winning the race, allowed a few photos to be taken, and in a rare departure from procedure, requested the microphone from the compere.

'Here we go!' Jim said excitedly to a bemused Joel.

'Ladies and gentlemen, I have a short announcement to make,' stated Lorrie with small smile. His voice seemed to boom around the track, bouncing off the walls of the century old buildings as he paused for a second or two.

'You have just witnessed my last ride as a professional jockey. I have recorded a thousand winners and I believe it's time for a change of direction. My retained yard and owners have been informed, and I have given up my rides in the last two races.'

This was received with a stony silence. Race-goers frowned at each other and racing hacks were immediately punching buttons on their mobile phones with frenetic abandon.

'From next week I will be moving from Newmarket and will be taking up residence in Malton at the Moorview Stables as a racehorse trainer. Myself and my Assistant Trainer, Mr Jim Wrigley, will immediately take charge of a dozen horses and I'm looking forward to this exciting new challenge.'

Handing the microphone back, Lorrie exited the winners' enclosure. He pushed his way past the gaggle of racing journalists desperate to secure an interview and arrived in front of Jim and Joel. Jim was beaming, whilst Joel was doing a fair impression of a goldfish, with wide, unblinking eyes whilst opening and closing his mouth without actually speaking.

'It seemed fitting to end my riding career here, and I needed the extra win to make it a true thousand,' he said simply.

'Pat Greene is now in his late sixties, but has taken out a license to train racehorses in Spain after eight years of retirement,' explained Jim, 'He gave up his lease in Malton and went abroad a few months after the La Duplicidad incident. Probably worried Lorrie would release the audio file.'

Lorrie took up the story, 'We think he's run out of money, so has started to train again. He will undoubtedly resume his old tricks of grooming young lads and lasses and then blackmailing them. We want you to write up our story as fiction. It's certainly got the plot of a racing thriller.'

'I agree,' Joel managed, nodding furiously.

'You should change the names and locations, but not what Pat did,' stated Jim.

Lorrie grinned darkly, 'However, we want you to leave in a number of small pointers. You know, little clues to who we're really talking about, so anyone working in the racing industry will be in no doubt who the story is based upon.'

'We'd like you to get it published in the Daily Racing News, or another racing journal, and possibly get it published as a novel, novella, or a short story. We plan to get it translated into Spanish and sent to the board of Sociedad de Fomento de la Cria Caballar de Espana, the racing authority over there,' Jim explained, 'If that doesn't get him stopped, we'll post links from social media and stir up enough interest from stable staff in Spain that will mean Pat will find it difficult to recruit.'

'And as an extra minor reward you will get the exclusive interview with me regarding my retirement from race riding and our plans to train,' Lorrie added.

Joel was reeling. An exclusive interview with the most talked about jockey retiring at the height of his career to become a trainer was a racing journalists dream assignment.

'Why me?' he asked, 'Why a relatively young reporter whose work you said yourself, didn't bear any relation to the trainer I'd just interviewed.'

Jim and Lorrie shared an amused look.

'I know the editor of your paper,' Jim revealed, 'I asked him to recommend a writer who was honest, and was capable of writing something with a hidden meaning. He told me about that interview. He told me the first version of your piece on Freddie Cartwright was a clever hatchet job where you carefully revealed the man's true colours, as long as you read between the lines. When he told you to water it down, your second version was even cleverer. In the end, he had to edit it himself, just in case Cartwright realised what you'd done and sued the paper. We liked your other work, and even though I pushed you on it earlier today, you didn't reveal to me what you'd originally written about Cartwright. All of this told us you were the man for our job.'

Joel took a deep breath, 'Well I'd best get on then. My editor is going to be breathing down my neck for this exclusive once he learns of your announcement.'

'Great!' Jim and Lorrie said in unison.

'Just one thing,' Joel added as the three men headed back to the winning connections room for a second time, 'Why did Pat Greene choose such an awful name for the filly?'

'Pat has been fined a number of times by the racing authorities, for all sorts of misdemeanours. He hates them with a vengeance, thinks they're out to get him – which is probably true. La Duplicidad isn't a Spanish restaurant at all, it simply means 'duplicity' or more accurately, 'the state of being double'. It was Pat's way of cocking a snook at the authorities, given he was using identical twin horses to cheat. It would have amused him.'

'Gentlemen,' Joel announced grandly, 'I think we've found the title to your short story.'

The Illingworth Experience

Five minutes ago, he'd looked on helplessly as a man died in this hospital room, thought Brian Hulme grimly.

It hadn't been a close relationship, it couldn't be really, given the circumstances, but still, they'd got on well. Brian supposed their mutual respect for each other could be classified as a friendship of sorts. He felt sadness, but it didn't feel like grief. However, the last twelve hours with Keith had been intense, and he supposed it was understandable if some emotions came bubbling up inside him.

Brian had been standing at the window of Keith's single, secure hospital room for perhaps half a minute, allowing his mind to wander. Presently he pressed his lips together and with growing sadness shook his head, before quietly drawing the curtains closed behind him. Above where Keith's bed had been, a gaudy digital wall clock flickered, drawing Brian's attention to the fact it was three minutes past four in the morning, its red numerals the brightest element in the dimly lit room. He blinked the numerals away and in doing so Brian experienced a sudden wave of tiredness.

Now that Keith's bed had been removed, along with its deceased occupant, the room felt cold and vacant. Only a couple of battered old chairs remained. The chatter was gone, and Keith's grin no longer warmed the immediate vicinity. The insistent ache in the small of Brian's back returned; it had been a long night.

With one arm bent at the elbow, Brian rubbed his lower back whilst he checked the room for any of Keith's personal effects he may have left behind. Having found a gnarled, well-thumbed novel and a pair of braces on the bedside table, Brian was about to check in with the doctor, when he studied the armchair where he been sitting, talking with Keith only a few minutes ago. That was before Keith suffered his second heart attack, the one that killed him. He breathed a low, long sigh.

They'd been the same age, or thereabouts… it wasn't fair to be dying in your fifties, not these days.

It was then that Brian remembered the folded sheaf of notepaper the kindly lady doctor had found on Keith before she'd pronounced him dead and taken him to the morgue. They were laid on his chair seat. He had to swallow hard when he read the words, 'For Brian Hulme, in the event of my death,' written on the front sheet in shaky capitals.

Then he remembered; Keith had asked for a pencil and a pad of paper earlier that evening, following the initial assessment upon their arrival at the hospital. He'd said he wanted to set a few things down by his own hand, just in case. He'd written for the best part of an hour, maybe two. Brian had assumed it would be a note to Keith's family, or a will of sorts. He never imagined it was a final note to himself.

With a heavy heart, Brian sat down and unfolded the pages…

Dear Mr Hulme,

I don't expect you to know this, Mr Hulme, but it was my birthday three months ago. I was fifty-five. I suppose that might explain why I began to think about Colin Illingworth and those six months I spent working with him in his betting shop in 1982. He was fifty-five when, like me, he had his dalliance with death.

I'll tell you right now Mr Hulme, or can I call you by your first name, Brian? I don't see why not. You see, I'm not one who has done much writing, Brian. You'll already know that I *like* talking – after all, we've whiled away many hours together in discussion… what I mean is, I've rarely actually sat down and *written*. Numbers always came much easier to me, so you'll have to forgive the miss-spellings(!) and my terrible grammar, (I'm particularly poor with the use of apostrophes') but I think I need to commit this one memory of mine to paper, as it may shine some light onto the events that have brought me to this hospital bed.

Anyway, on with my story. I was seventeen, almost eighteen in the winter of 1982, and after failing my A-levels through boredom, (and a significant lack of application) I somehow found out that a small independent bookmaker in a local town was on the lookout for a lad to mark the board. I'd always been fascinated by odds and the analysis of horseracing form, ever since I'd attended a jumps meeting at Wetherby when I was seven.

My interview at Illingworth Turf Accountants consisted of Colin, the wiry, wild-haired and pinched-faced proprietor, eyeing me suspiciously through the steel mesh glass that protected the counter. Early eighties bookmaking shops were more like wild west saloons, being smoke-filled, windowless, dirty, and often the counter service would consist of a small letterbox sized gap surrounded by reinforced glass embedded with a metal grid. You would slide your two-part betting slip into the gap, along with your stake and it would be processed by a cashier, usually with a cigarette hanging from their lips.

Colin proceeded to ask me what my father did for a living, and after giving an affirming nod at the answer, demanded I count from twenty-five backwards to zero in less than twenty seconds. With this task completed, he unbolted the counter door, complete with a shatter-safe window kept in place by masking tape, and invited me into his domain. Handing over two marker pens, one red, the other blue he indicated the raised plinth below the odds board with his eyes and I stepped up three feet and marked the odds up for the last two races at Monmore and then Wimbledon dogs.

It was simple enough, relaying the odds given over the blower. I'm sure you might remember bookies in the early eighties, but if not, the blower was a small speaker through which the well-spoken commentators communicated odds and commentaries - this was well before TV screens and those soulless betting machines were allowed in bookies. Colin's blower was yellowed by years of stagnant cigarette smoke, and it buzzed incessantly when no one was speaking. I dutifully transposed the changing odds onto the grey, pre-printed paper race lists, attaching them to the steel-backed board with magnetic strips, and ensuring the favourite's odds in each race were marked in red, and the rest in blue. I'd been visiting my local betting shop since I was sixteen, so knew the drill. As long as I could prove I had a sharp ear, quick writing skills, and knew the difference between 85/40 and 9/4, I would be a shoe-in. That's as long as he didn't ask my age...

Eight minutes later Colin told me, 'I'll give yer a pound fifty an hour, cash in hand, no tax or that sort of nonsense. You get paid on Friday nights and if I find yer fingers in me till I'll 'av 'em off.' I was instructed to return the next day and to be ready for the first show at one o'clock in time for the start of Newbury's afternoon race-meeting at one-fifteen.

So began my introduction to bookmaking. Being the only betting shop in a town of three thousand people, it was a busy little place. In those days, your local bookie's was the only place to strike a bet, so the fact the shop was damp, shabby, windowless, and reeked of stale smoke, made no difference. In a way, I suppose it may well have enhanced the experience for many of the punters. Having a bet in a bookies was like entering a busy nightclub, where all of life was on show.

I reckon we've lost the joy of pitching yourself against a bookmaker to whom you could put a face and name. With mobile phones, a gambling device is in your pocket at all times now, and I find internet betting with one of the faceless betting corporations a desperate experience.

It was a complete experience in the eighties. Illingworth Turf Accountants had a small bell located at the top of the doorframe, and it jingled all morning and much of the afternoon as customers came and went, and I soon got to know many of the punters on first name terms.

Colin kept me on the odds board for the first few days.

On the first Wednesday, he gruffly announced he would allow me to take bets, having worked out that I could calculate doubles and trebles in my head. Within a fortnight, I was settling simple bets and paying them out between betting shows and balancing the till at the end of the evening. There was no night racing, no racing twenty-four hours a day – by law we had to shut fifteen minutes after the last race of the afternoon.

As the months passed, I got to know Colin and discovered his constantly grumpy persona was simply an act he put on for his customers. The suspicious hardening of his eyes when he took a bet of more than a fiver and sighs of contempt as he paid out a large bet was pure theatre. He played up to his audience, ensuring that whether the punters won or lost, they were sure to return.

But when Colin disappeared into the back of the shop – into his inner sanctum – the *real* Colin emerged. A family man with two teenage children and a wife with whom he constantly bickered, Colin's real love was for his horseracing. I can still see him, perched on a high stool in the middle of the back office with a fly swatter in his hand, whacking his hip every now and again as he animatedly pretended to ride to the sound of the commentary coming over the blower, encouraging the right result to drop for him. On one occasion - trying to get a big loser for the shop beat - he became so immersed in driving his imaginary mount to the winning line, he became unbalanced, got his feet tangled up in his stool, and fell off before the race had finished. He landed awkwardly on the back room floor, spraining his ankle. However, he was laughing that hard he didn't notice his injury until he tried to stand up. All credit to him, he stood on one leg, still chuckling, until the result of the photo finish came through, and cheered at the news that the result had gone his way before he complained about the pain.

Colin was certainly a fair businessman, although I doubt his bank manager, the racing authorities, or the VAT man would agree. He deposited cash regularly at the local Barclays, but never more than a few hundred pounds per week. Instead, the safe in his office would bulge with cash until the last week of every month, whereupon his profits would magically disappear, along with the bets he'd neglected to put through the till for certain, high staking clients, so the bets didn't qualify for any levy, or tax payment. There was a small back garden behind the betting shop and once a month Colin would wink at me, tell me to hold the fort, and depart out the back door with a box of matches and a shoebox filled with betting slips that had failed to make it through the till.

It was this build-up of cash in the safe during the month, and his meagre deposits at the bank that was probably responsible for what happened on Boxing Day. It had been a busy afternoon; in those days there could easily be ten to fifteen meetings on a Bank Holiday and we'd been inundated with bets. It was four forty-five, with the last race at Kempton having run ten minutes previously. The shop was now empty, with the last punter having just left. Screwed up betting slips littered the small bet-writing shelf that ran around the punters area, some of the newspapers I'd pinned to the wall in the morning were ripped and marked with biro, and the floor was strewn with losing slips mixed in with damp, muddy footprints. Colin was in the back room, totting up the few telephone bets he took each day. I was on my way across the to the door, key in hand, when it opened a crack and the little bell above it tinkled.

'Sorry, we're closing. You can collect any winnings tomorrow,' I called out as I reached for the door handle in order to apologise and, if necessary, explain further.

A green woollen face with swimming goggles for eyes poked around the door. Behind the bluey plastic, a pair of long eyelashes blinked at me.

Two medium-sized men wearing overalls and similar woollen masks burst into the shop. Startled, I took a few steps backwards and there was that moment – you'll know the one, Mr Hulme – where you size up the true extent of the problem you're now suddenly faced with. I was surprised to find I wasn't scared; in fact, I became incredibly focused, though it may have had something to do with the fact that both men were waving the barrels of serious looking guns towards me.

The second chap pushed a firm, leather gloved hand into my chest, sending me back a few more yards whilst his blue-goggled accomplice waited behind. He repeated the action until I bumped into the bet writing shelf on the far side wall.

'On your knees and be quiet,' he rasped, and I complied immediately, folding myself down onto the worn yellow and blue vinyl tiles. He lifted his shotgun and I can remember stealing a glance up and inspecting the weapon curiously, wondering why the barrels pointed at my face were two shiny, ragged steel rings. I soon realised they'd been hacksawed off, rather inexpertly by the look of it. He screamed something else at me - I didn't have a clue what he said - he had a rather weak voice and I couldn't catch everything from behind his knitted woollen bobble-hat whose brim had had been unfolded so it reached his chin. Two slits had been cut for his eyes, through which the swimming goggles protruded.

When I shrugged, and said I couldn't understand, he tried again, with a single word hissed under his breath, 'Key!'

'In my hand,' I told him sweetly.

Then he did something that made my blood run cold. My aggressor rolled his eyes contemptuously. And I knew. Behind the children's plastic swimming goggles, his brown eyes completed their rotation and I could picture the sneer that always accompanied this affectation, hidden beneath his bobble hat. I knew who he was. And by association, I immediately realised who the long lashes belonged to. The lad pointing his gun at me was Si Cookham and behind him was his amiable, but downtrodden friend, Jeff Taylor. A pair of small-staking local lads who frequented the shop on a regular basis were, stupidly, conducting an armed robbery of their local bookies.

'Give the key here!' Si growled lightly with an open palm. I handed it over.

Jeff was passed the key and duly secured the door, leaving it in the lock.

Si poked the muzzle of his gun into my shoulder, 'Colin in the back?'

'Who?' I asked innocently.

'You know who!' Si spat, the outline of his mouth suddenly pulling at the threads of his hat.

Si was a poor gambler, a bad loser, and unpredictable. Colin had ordered him out of the shop on a few occasions, usually after a run of bad luck that plunged Si into an act of frustrated aggression. Slamming his fist into an inanimate object several times such as a wall or bench was his favourite reaction, combined with an expletive ridden rant. With his gun levelled between my eyes, I accepted defeat and indicated the open counter door and a further closed door that led to Colin's lair, the back office.

Si snorted beneath his mask and stalked off, entering the back office like a raging bull, after leaving Lorrie in no doubt that should I move a muscle he was to, 'Splatter his brains across the form for the 3-35pm at Uttoxeter.'

Jeff and I heard a shout, then talking in the back office, followed by silence. A long minute and a half later a shaken looking Colin appeared at the back office door. I noticed he was wearing his jacket, and wondered whether Si had dropped lucky, and caught him transferring the cash to his pockets in order to take it to… wherever it went.

'You okay?' I called to him.

'Yeah, I'm fine…' he replied in a thoroughly disgusted voice, then noticing Jeff holding his shotgun to my head he vociferously added, '…and *what the hell* are you doing to my board marker?'

Without a thought for his own safety, Colin bustled through the counter door, suddenly red-faced and angry.

'How dare the two of you burst in here! And as for you, pointing that... disgusting gun at him!' he complained as he strode into the punters' area, gesticulating and somehow managing to stamp his feet as he crossed the floor. He caught Jeff off-guard and grabbing the end of his gun, pointed it away from me and up towards the ceiling.

'You going to kill someone for a few grand?' Colin shouted into the lad's face.

'Stop right there, old man,' Si warned in a cocky tone behind him.

He'd followed Colin out of the back room and was now nonchalantly swinging his shotgun inexpertly around in one hand. In the other, a striped Jacksons supermarket carrier bag was bulging with banknotes, each wrapped with an elastic band in bundles of a hundred pounds.

'I said *stop*, old man!'

Old!' Colin protested, rounding on Si, 'I'll... I'll...'

'You'll do what?' Si said sarcastically. He'd lodged the gun's butt under his right arm and was gesticulating wildly with it, taunting Colin with his mastery of the weapon, 'You gunna fight me for the money, you old crock?'

Colin didn't answer. He'd gone very white and his mouth had suddenly twisted into a rictus of pain.

'My chest is tight. I don't... feel too well. I'm going to...' he gurgled, staggering towards Si with his arms out, imploring the lad to catch him.

Colin half tripped, half fell headlong onto Si. The two of them crashed to the floor in a tangle of arms, legs, plastic bag, and shotgun. Si started swearing, scrabbling to get to his feet, but hindered by Colin's long, thin arms and legs.

Without warning, an almighty crack shook the shop. Si lay motionless for a moment, then lifted his eyes to peer up at the ceiling tile that had just exploded above us all. Blobs of white polystyrene fell to the shop floor, mixed with shredded betting slips. Larger bits of the tarnished ceiling tile soon lay there, along with the shotgun and the Jackson's bag Si had dropped in terror.

Colin was the first to speak. He'd struggled to his feet
'I'm not feeling too... arrgh!'

His eyes suddenly glazed and his knees wobbled. He gazed, glassy-eyed at me for a moment. Then I watched in horror as Colin's breaths became gasps and he began to paw, then clutch at his chest. He staggered drunkenly around Si on the floor, who was seemingly unable to move, transfixed by the ailing bookmaker. Colin gave an imploring, breathless squeak and still desperately clawing at his chest, as if trying to tear it apart, he crumpled, landing face-down onto the hard floor with a sickening thump, causing a wave of discarded betting slips to be wafted into the air.

Si was sitting beside Colin's inert body, hugging his arms around himself and even with his goggles on, I could see his eyes were wide with fright.

'Bloody Hell!' Jeff complained bitterly in a tiny, scared voice, 'I told you not to load the guns. You've gone and killed him!'

I went to Colin and fell to my knees, feeling for a pulse on the nape of his neck, and turned to the two would-be robbers and confirmed there was no pulse.

With that, Jeff leapt to the door and after fumbling with the key for a few seconds, wrenched the shop door open and without uttering another word or looking over his shoulder at his partner, disappeared into the evening gloom. The departure of his accomplice spurred Si into action. He scrambled to his feet, his eyes darting from me and then to the body face down on the floor. He stooped, picked up his gun and I wondered for one awful moment whether he was contemplating using it on me. He looked down at Colin's prone body once more, clenched a fist, and swore loudly. His decision made, he too bolted out of the shop.

As soon as Si was gone, I jumped up, slammed the shop

door shut, locking and bolting it top and bottom. I swung around… and was met by the sight of Colin sitting on the floor with a big grin on his face, and holding out a hand to me so he could be pulled to his feet.

All it had taken was a wink. One small, split second movement of his eyelid my way after the gun had gone off and Colin not only enacted a way out of the situation, he'd also communicated it to me. I just played along. He'd also made sure he'd fallen squarely onto the carrier bag full of his money, guessing the two lads wouldn't want to roll a corpse over to get at their booty.

Colin took the whole episode in his stride. He repaired the roof himself that night with some spare tiles and the shop opened as usual at ten-thirty the next morning. He saw to it that Si and Jeff had the fear of god put into them by a couple of far more serious villains the next day. It was soon after that Colin revealed he'd enjoyed a rather checkered past himself, and still knew a few 'faces' from the local crime scene.

As for me, I was fine until I got home that night, whereupon I had a bout of delayed shock and needed several pints at my local to steady my shaking hands.

So as I was saying earlier, I got to thinking about Colin on my fifty-fifth birthday three months ago. And those thoughts led to me reassess Colin's actions on that December evening in 1982.

You see Mr Hulme, my father was a company accountant. After a few more enjoyable months with Colin, I re-sat and passed my A-Levels and at a loss as to what to do, I followed my father's lead. I went to study the art of accounting at university. Fifteen years later, I found myself doing quite well as the Financial Director of a national bookmaking chain. However, I decided they weren't treating me right, or rewarding me for the err… *artistic* way in which I handled their revenues, profits and tax calculations. Like Colin, I learned the system back to front, and so I began to bleed my company of small, hardly noticeable amounts of money, that I managed to weasel into dozens of bank accounts. Over the years, it built up into quite a tidy little sum. With investment and interest gains I amassed over twenty million pounds.

When the company finally caught me, they considered not reporting the theft. After all, it didn't reflect too well on them. They'd not noticed my pilfering every month for fifteen years… but in the end they decided to go public and reported me to the police. Of course, not long after, I met you, Mr Hulme. And as prison guards go, you've exceeded my expectations!

You'll be aware that I'm serving a twelve year sentence for the crime of embezzlement. With good behaviour I might get out after a decade, as I refused to tell the authorities where the money was hidden, and my self-righteous judge recommended I serve a minimum term of ten years. The reason for this? Well, he pointed to me not displaying any remorse, or indeed any indication of contrition towards the wronged party. The *wronged party*… I ask you! Since when did any bookmaker require a show of remorse? They just gambled that it would be worth the bad publicity in order to get their twenty million back. I wasn't about to give them the satisfaction! And I'm not about to wait around for another nine and a half years to spend my money either.

After having spent two months researching heart attacks, and what doctors look for when assessing such cases, I set about feigning a number of small 'events' that led the prison doctor to believe I was suffering from mild angina. Finally, this evening, when I knew the medical facility at the prison would be un-manned, and that you would be guarding the midnight watch on my wing, I pretended to suffer a major attack, ensuring all the primary signs would be present. I even did so in front of you, Brian, in order to be certain it would be *you* that accompanied me as I was rushed to the nearest hospital with the correct facilities – this hospital, in fact. I made sure the timings would work in my favour; the shift change for the overnight doctors, and at a time where the accident and emergency would be busy with the Saturday night/Sunday morning rush of alcohol related injuries. So long as I looked to be out of any immediate life-threatening trouble I knew I'd be monitored overnight, but with a minimal amount of attention dedicated to me.

Finally, to my dying swan routine on my death bed... I will wait until only you and I are in the secure room they use for prisoners like me. I do hope you enjoyed the show, I imagine I'll be clasping my hands to my chest just like Colin did all those years ago. When that junior doctor came in, pronounced me dead, and carted me off to the morgue, I'd like to think you shed a tear... if so, I'll have made Colin proud.

You see, with twenty million pounds readily available to me, finding a young, good-looking, confident woman doctor to walk by at the right moment when no other medical staff are around, wearing a white coat and telling the prison officer with me that, unfortunately this patient has suffered a huge heart attack and has unfortunately died... is terribly easy. I noticed that you always allow that pretty young prison officer, Ms Jones, I think she's called, to run rings around you. Having a weakness for a pretty face is why I chose you.

I imagine my fake doctor will advise you to take a few minutes to yourself, in order to recover from the emotional stress my death caused you? Either way, during that time, I will have made a miraculous recovery and headed for the hospital exit, and a waiting car to whisk me away.

I thought hard about that evening when Colin and I were faced with the robbery, and like him, I needed to use *a distraction*. You see, it wasn't Si's gun that went off... Colin always kept a gun in his office drawer; a starting pistol filled with shredded paper. Meant to scare and not cause any serious injury. When he staggered across towards Si, clutching at his heart, he reached into his jacket, pulled out the gun and once they had both tumbled to the ground, he pointed it at the ceiling. He'd manufactured the entire scene to scare the young robbers away.

And my great distraction?

It's this letter of course, Brian. Not all distractions have to go bang! I've seen you, reading your crime thrillers at your desk in the prison during the long nights… I have calculated that reading my recollections of Colin Illingworth will have taken you close to twenty-two minutes, by which time… I will be long gone.

Farewell, and thanks, Brian,

Keith.

PS. I suggest you destroy my note. Should your employers read it, I can't imagine they will be too forgiving.

Speedy Genes

Jonathan Porter watched in fascination as the thread of blood flowing from the young man's head began to congeal among the straw and sawdust on the stable floor. A familiar sense of unworldliness crept over him, breaking his concentration, and he reminded himself that there was no need to panic.

Suddenly aware he must have been standing over the corpse for five, maybe six minutes, he shook his head violently. He would need his senses to be sharp and all his guile to repair the damage from that one moment of insan…

No! it wasn't insanity he told himself, it was… he searched for the words… entirely logical given his understandable concern, yes, that was it - concern for himself, his employees, his clients… and for the entire worldwide racehorse breeding industry worth billions! That understandable concern had led to a split second of entirely logical… rage. The tears of self-pity, the feeling of fear, and finally, desperation that he'd succumbed to immediately afterwards were nothing more than shock. He wasn't a violent man, nor was he prone to sudden impulses… And yet, he had grasped the young scientist's annoyingly long curly hair in both hands, twisted him around and beaten his head against the porcelain trough until it had smashed…

Porter winced, feeling rising bile from his stomach sting the base of his throat. A tingle of fear began to invade his body once more, jangling through his nerves.

'I'm in control,' he muttered to himself in an attempt to cast both his worries, and their physical manifestation, away. Following a series of deep breaths, Porter held the air in, then blew it out, allowing his cheeks to inflate as he exhaled, and forced himself to concentrate.

'I am the Managing Director of the biggest bloodstock sales company in Britain,' he told the bay colt that was sharing the stable with him, 'I'm alone in one of the hundreds of stables used on a sale day. But today is not a sale day. There are only a handful of lots left on the premises from the yearling sale we hosted two days ago, and virtually all the staff are in the offices.'

The young horse with a milky white blaze down its forehead stared dolefully at Porter, then pawed the floor with its front leg.

'You're the only one who knows the truth,' Porter stated quietly to the young horse. The colt snorted restlessly and turned its back on him, carefully avoiding touching the prone man on the floor.

'Don't be like that. I had to stop him!' Porter said reproachfully, 'If anyone else had seen what he could do... well, *you'd* be for the chop for a start!'

Porter leaned his back against the stable door for a moment, then slid to the floor where he sat, holding his knees. He needed time to think, he decided. He should consider what brought him to this stable and that would help determine his next course of action.

***

2-00pm - One and a quarter hours earlier.

With his glass office walls, Porter spotted the unkempt, gangly, curly haired youth as he climbed the stairs to his second-floor office. He groaned inwardly and wondered why he'd agreed with his deputy, John Westerly, to see this... his name was Cunning-something or other. Then he remembered recent events and how Westerly had protected him when he'd experienced a moment of... indiscipline. His Deputy Managing Director had been insistent that this lad was worth giving up some time to hear him out. He apparently had a technical device of some sort… so he'd allowed Westerly to book this young chap into his diary for fifteen minutes, simply in order to pacify him; he owed him this much.

Unshaven and with a curtain of hair constantly requiring to be a flicked away from his eyes, the lad - he couldn't be more than twenty years old – entered his office without knocking and carefully placed his rucksack beside the chair in front of Porter's expansive desk. Porter leaned back languidly and tried to smile over at the grinning youth who hadn't offered his hand to shake, but found it challenging to disguise his distaste. The boy saw fit to wear trainers, faded jeans, and a tour t-shirt for some rock band to a business meeting, so Porter could only manage a thin-lipped grimace. Tradition was one of the cornerstones of this bloodstock business.

'I'm extremely busy, Mr…'

'Cunningham, Saul Cunningham,' the boy interjected happily, 'Yes, I appreciate you'll be busy after the five-day yearling sale, but I think…'

'Indeed, I understand you *think* you have a…' Porter paused to smile condescendingly at the student thirty-five years his younger, '…*revolutionary* invention.'

'Yeah, I *think* I do,' the boy replied with slow determination, locking eyes with the businessman. He studied the older man for a moment and his grin faded when Porter inexplicably leaned over and flicked one of the central silver balls in a Newton's Cradle that occupied pride of place in the corner of his desk. The mechanism was sitting upon a plinth inset with a small brass plaque announcing it had been presented to Porter by a member of the Saudi Royal Family. Each silver orb was engraved with a horse's head. The Director seemed confused when the ball didn't elicit his anticipated respinse, staring at the game with a heavily creased forehead. Saul remained silent as Porter lost interest, leaned back in his chair, steepled his hands, and zoned back in on him.

'Fire away then!' Porter barked.

'Listen, if you're not interested, I can…'

'Nonsense! We may be over a hundred and fifty years old, but we're a bloodstock sales company with an eye to the future,' Porter assured him jovially, 'Why, we even allow owners to place bids online now.'

'Yeah, about five years after your biggest competitor. You know, on reflection I think this may have been a bad idea…'

'There you go, *thinking* again!' Porter enthused, starting to enjoy himself, 'Come on, just tell me what you've got, I'm listening.'

Saul stared with slightly narrowed eyes at the Managing Director. There was something about the man's left eye that wasn't quite right… and it unnerved him. But he had travelled for two hours to get here, so he might as well practice his pitch…

'It's nothing too earth-shattering really,' Saul shrugged, 'I can predict the ability of racehorses before they race.'

Porter smiled knowingly, 'So you've got a ratings system based on past form and pedigree?'

Saul shook his head, 'No, through a combination of measurements and gene matching I can predict whether a racehorse will be successful or not.'

The Director rolled his eyes and Saul made to get up.

'I'm sorry,' Porter said lightheartedly, waving Saul back down onto his seat, 'You're undoubtedly an intelligent lad, and I don't doubt you have worked hard on this theory of yours, but hundreds of years of experience have told us that equine pedigree and physique are the only true indicators of a young racehorses' potential. The bloodstock industry is built on those foundations.'

'Not any more,' Saul replied stoically, 'And I can prove it.'

'Away you go then… do your stuff,' Porter said with a sad smile. Consulting his watch he added, 'The floor is yours for… seven minutes.'

Saul bit the inside of his mouth, not sure whether he shouldn't just walk out. This Managing Director was acting oddly, and indeed, his bloodstock company was clearly stuck in the past. John Westerly, the Deputy Director he'd originally spoken with had seemed to understand what he'd achieved, but he doubted either man would ever really tap the potential in what he'd discovered through three years of research and development. Even so, the opportunity to put this puffed up old duffer in his place was simply too great.

From out of his rucksack, Saul removed a laptop and a device that to Porter, looked like a set of electric curling tongs with a USB connector at the end of the wire instead of a plug.

'Really?' he asked sarcastically, 'Is that how your hair gets like that?'

'Please stand up,' said Saul, ignoring the comment.

Opening his laptop, Saul plugged the tongs into the side of the device and placed it on the desk. He rattled his fingers across the keyboard for a few seconds before turning to his subject expectantly, 'Arm's up,' he ordered.

Porter rolled his eyes again, but did as he was told. The tongs, or wand, as he now realised the device more closely resembled, was passed over his chest, around under his arms and finally over his back. The boy tapped on his keyboard a few times and then turned the laptop to show an image.

'That's your heart,' he said, 'In three dimensions. I can tell you that it's slightly under the average size for a human of your height and weight.'

Porter peered at the laptop screen. A green outline of a heart was displayed along with a wide range of measurements.

'Impressive,' he said with a raised eyebrow, 'But I don't see…'

Saul hit another key on the laptop, 'That's your throat and trachea. You'll be pleased to learn it's perfectly normal. However, if you were a racehorse…'

Saul hit another key, '…I would never buy you because you're going to be slow. As slow as it's possible for a horse to be according to this report. So it's a good job you're human.'

Porter bent over and examined the small laptop screen for a few more seconds and then straightened.

'So you can measure the size of a horse's heart… so what? It doesn't mean it can run quickly.'

'I'm afraid it rather does,' Saul rebuffed, closing his laptop and placing it back in his rucksack, 'A combination of the heart and lung sizes, the height, length of the horse, the width of the palate and trachea combines to give a very accurate determination. And then there's the overlay of gene analysis to determine whether they have the DNA that indicates flight potential, or the *speedy genes*, as I like to call them.'

'You took blood samples of each racehorse?' Porter queried, trying to keep the horror from his voice.

Saul curled his lip at him, 'You think I would stick a syringe in all of those yearlings whilst the vendor was standing watching?'

Porter didn't reply, remaining poker-faced.

'No,' he sighed irritably, 'All I needed to do was take one of the horse's hairs, process it in a portable device I've developed called the 'Gene Machine', and examine the result to discover if each racehorse possesses the speedy gene.'

Porter began to feel a little light-headed. This lad was in a fantasy land, he had to be, 'The *speedy* gene?' he repeated sarcastically.

'The speedy gene,' the lad repeated, 'Took me all three years of my BA and a year and a half of my PhD, but I finally got there. I've managed to find the markers on a horse's DNA that tell you whether they are built to race quickly.'

Watching the young man pack away, Porter was silent for a few seconds. He was still standing, and now pointed to the rucksack, 'You can take that wand thing, and know all those measurements from inside a horse's body from just walking around it?'

'Exactly as I did with you. I also take a hair sample to confirm they have the correct markers in their genome, but that's a thirty second job…'

Saul had just caught a look at the Director's face and his voice trailed off. It seemed Mr Porter had undergone something of a change of heart.

'But this is untested isn't it. You're just guessing. You've not tried this with er… live subjects…'

The boy gave him a slightly contemptuous look, 'I've been attending your yearling sales for the last two years. I have data that proves I can rate a racehorse to within a statistically high degree of accuracy.'

Saul watched a variety of expressions flit across the Director's features until it settled into thoughtful determination.

'I don't suppose you have that proof here with you?'

Saul paused, trying to read the older man. It was now obvious he'd managed to grab Porter's attention, but he wasn't so sure he would be the type to help him develop his system.

'It would simply help me to sell the concept to my fellow directors,' Porter said to fill the void when the lad didn't answer, 'I was perhaps a little hasty in my initial assessment of you.. er.. *your* invention, but as you can imagine, the racing industry, and more accurately, the bloodstock business has operated in the same way for a very long time. What I've seen today is… well, nothing short of miraculous, if you can back it up with hard statistics.'

Saul dug into a separate pocket of his rucksack, removed a bulky document, found a specific page, and showed Porter a diagram with notations.

'My results from last year's yearling sales at the top three sales companies. I scanned a random sample of a hundred horses at each sale and ranked them. Then I waited until the end of their 2YO seasons and correlated my own findings to their official ratings.'

Porter inspected the graphical evidence and as he read a numbness spread from his fingers, up his arms and then shot down his legs. His knees began to buckle and he grabbed the desk and eased himself onto it. According to the figures in front of him, the boy's method had correctly identified a number of the top-performing horses that had passed through his sales ring last year. What was more amazing, was that he'd managed to identify a number of top performers that had gone through the sales ring for only a few thousand guineas.

'I need to see you use your gadget on a real horse,' said Porter.

2-45pm

'You're serious? You can envisage how my technology can be incorporated into the process of evaluating the racehorses you sell?'

Saul was quizzing the Director as he led him down yet another dusty lane with long terraces of stables either side.

'Absolutely! We will need to evaluate your methodology ourselves of course, but I can see it could alter the way racehorses are sold!' Porter remarked, playfully clapping the lad around his shoulders, sending himself slightly off-balance and having to steady himself.

Saul took a sidelong glance at his host and nearly said something, stalling as he drew to a halt.

'Here we are, the isolation boxes,' Porter declared, 'We can try your gadget out on this yearling. He's due to fly out to America tomorrow so is being held here until he's ready to go.'

The stable door was closed both top and bottom. Porter drew back a bolt in the centre of the door and kicked at the steel latch at the bottom, missing twice before it wheeled back, allowing them to peer into a good-sized, dimly lit stable. A young horse eyed the two men suspiciously as they entered his space.

'Okay, show me how it's done,' Porter prompted, wringing his hands and grinning.

The poor light shadowed the Directors face and Saul paused, unable to decide whether he was displaying excitement or apprehension. Glancing around the stable he noted it was bare apart from a water bowl on the wall and a small window measuring no more than a foot square. The window faced the yard but only allowed a bare minimum of light to enter the box, being set behind iron bars and encrusted with years of dust and grime. Cobwebs dominated the walls and ceiling and the heavy, vegetable odour of horse droppings hung in the dry, dusty air. He glanced back at Porter and found him wide-eyed and expectant. I'll get this done quickly, Saul told himself as he set about removing his kit from his rucksack.

Once he was ready, Saul turned to Porter, who had silently been following every stage of his setup. A flash of movement behind the small window caught his eye for a moment, but he ignored it – it would be a stable lad or suchlike. He was keen to get this over with as quickly as possible, and soon ran through the heart, valves, and wind scan and subsequent analysis on his laptop. As he worked, Porter asked only two questions from the other side of the stable, about the gene analysis, and the alacrity of those results. Saul had replied that the gene cross-check in the laboratory took twenty-four hours, but that the initial set of findings regarding the heart, lungs, and palate, along with his portable speedy gene checker could be revealed in minutes.

During the scan Saul was unable to flush certain thoughts about the Director from his mind. His odd movements, the loss of balance, and his slightly garbled language... but it wasn't his place. Perhaps a word with the other Director he'd seen earlier might...

'And so... that's it, isn't it?' Porter said with arms crossed, 'Tell me, Saul, how do you r-r-rate this colt?'

66

'No, we're not finished Mr Porter. I need to do the gene analysis… I told you that only a few minutes ago.'

Porter stared at the young man for a long moment before mumbling something incomprehensible whilst bending over and rubbing his forehead. He felt light-headed and his palms were sweaty.

'Tell me then… how did the colt score?' Porter demanded.

'Er… well, to be frank, he's never going to be racehorse of any note. His heart is smaller than it should be for a horse of his size and one of his lungs is only operating at about seventy-five percent capacity. I predict he will need a wind operation within the next eighteen months as well.'

Porter screwed his face up. Saul was uncertain what this meant; the man looked to be in pain.

'We sold this colt as a top prospect with a clean set of veterinary reports. It was bought by a high profile American syndicate for eight-hundred thousand guineas,' he whispered, 'What do you think this horse would be worth if they heard what you'd just said?'

Saul pushed his lips out and stared at the ground for a moment before answering, 'I imagine they would choose another racehorse. That's the beauty of my invention buyers would be far better informed…'

'Only the best horses would ever get sold!' Porter cried, 'Our *vendors* are the most important people to an auction house. You would immediately reduce our revenues by, by… two thirds!'

'That would only be a short-term effect,' Saul countered, 'With this technology you would ensure only the best animals, the sires with no inherent defects, the mares possessing the speedy gene, would be used for…'

'And in the meantime, we go out of business! What you've invented is a surefire way of removing sales companies from the supply chain… Vendors will do your little test and *know* when they have a world-beating horse and either keep it, or go straight to the half a dozen people rich enough to afford to pay the millions it is worth. The rest won't even bother selling their horses...'

Porter had gone red in the face, and for a few seconds started to fight for his breath.

'Do you feel okay, Mr Porter? You appear to be a little unwell, if you don't mind me...'

Porter raised his head and Saul froze. The Director was baring his teeth and a snarl of barely controlled madness came rumbling up through his throat. Beside him, the colt whinnied nervously and jig-jogged around to face Porter.

Backing away, Saul held up two flat palms, 'I've been working with genes for the last four years...'

'You are the d-d-devil dressed in s-student clothes! With your long hair...'

I believe you may be suffering from early onset dementia, Mr Porter!' Saul shouted above the Director's garbled accusations, 'You need to calm down, Sir.'

'How *dare* you!'

Saul stood his ground, 'You can't speak properly, your short-term memory is shot, you're getting disoriented. You can't even start a Newton's Cradle for crying out loud! You flicked the second ball in the line... outwards!'

Porter's eyes appeared to bulge and his brows shot up his forehead.

'These are all classic symptoms of dementia. You really need to see a doctor and you certainly shouldn't be at work...' continued Saul. Porter had balled his fists and he was shaking uncontrollably with a searing rage.

'Get out. Take your stuff and go!' Porter hissed, sending a cloud of spittle into the dead air in the stable.

Saul hurriedly nodded and turned to retrieve his rucksack.

Porter, his hands shaking, straightened his back and rushed at Saul as he bent over in the back of the stable. He took two large handfuls of his hair, and summoning every ounce of strength Porter slammed the boy's head against the porcelain water trough attached to the stable wall.

3-17pm

A knock on the stable door made no impression on Porter, he remained sitting on the cold concrete floor, hugging his knees and rocking slightly.

'Porter, Are you in there?'

He recognised the far-off voice somewhere behind him, but couldn't place it. Right now Porter was more worried about the large, yellow-toothed monster that was bearing down on him. It's acrid breath smelled of long dead vegetables and as for its long, engorged tongue... he winced, covering his face with his hands as the monster snorted onto his head once more and its lips tugged at his hair.

Without warning he was thrust forward. The stable door was pushed inwards and the silhouette of a small man brandishing a mucking out fork filled the frame. Sunlight pouring into the stable around the figure who remained motionless for a long moment with Porter squinting up at him.

'I.. er, he was...' Porter mumbled, getting to his feet.

'What the hell have you done, Porter?' croaked Westerly, aghast at the sight of the broken drinking trough and the young lad laid awkwardly beneath. There was an unnatural, foreboding atmosphere emanating from the stable. Even the colt seemed somewhat cowed, studying Westerly with ears flat against the side of its head.

Westerly leaned the fork against the stable wall, took out his mobile phone, and began punching in numbers.

3-47pm

Westerly stood with three other members of his staff, behind a small cordoned-off area watching Porter being helped into a police car.

'I thought he was acting a bit funny the last few weeks,' Mary, the Managing Directors secretary commented airily.

'Really, I hadn't noticed,' Westerly responded in a thoughtful tone.

'I mean, he'd started to forget things, like his glasses and his car keys,' she gossiped, 'And I found him humming a tune at his desk the other day, Mr Porter has *never* hummed in all the twenty years I've worked with him!'

They fell silent as Porter stared balefully out of the car window as he was slowly driven away. He appeared to Westerly to be oddly serene.

'I heard the word *dementia* being mentioned a few times by the ambulance staff,' Westerly commented with a calculated hint of sadness in his voice. The gaggle of office staff around him nodded or mumbled expressions of understanding.

4-15pm

Westerly was sitting in the Managing Directors office, regarding with muted amusement all the items he would be removing and replacing. The old man's awards would be first. His predecessor had cluttered the office with personal memorabilia from all three decades of his reign, whereas Westerly preferred a clean, sharp environment to work within. He could do without the distractions of the past. Once he'd made the calls to report Porter's actions, the board had immediately asked him to stand in, as he knew they would. Tradition was a hard habit to break. However, as he pressed his back into the old man's seat it somehow felt uncomfortable, as if Porter had left an unshakeable imprint that would only ever suit his frame. Westerly decided the chair would have to go too.

Saul's body hadn't been taken out of the stable yet. Westerly imagined this was police standard practice, after all, there had been a murder, or manslaughter at the very least… although the forensic team hadn't arrived yet. It could be a long night.

Out in the corridor, a knot of employees was huddled around the one window on the second floor that provided an uninterrupted view of the stable. The walls of the Managing Directors office were glass – Porter had believed you should be able to see what everyone was doing and rarely closed the blinds – so Westerly had been keeping an eye on the small group, leaving his door open so he could hear their comments. He'd accepted the gawping for the last hour, but now decided to move them on. As he rose from his chair, the stretching of necks and jostling for position became more urgent.

'Ooh, look, they're bringing a young lad out,' said one of the canteen staff , 'That looks promising though, it looks like he's just had a bang on the head!'

Westerly's blood ran cold. He recovered quickly, but left the office and walked to the window with his heart thumping in his chest; far quicker than when he'd been outside the stable, taking sneaky looks through that small, square window.

With a sharp comment, Westerly cut through the cluster of people at the window and watched in utter horror as the ambulance crew brought a heavily bandaged Saul out on a collapsible trolley. He'd been waiting for a body bag to emerge from the stable, not this… if he'd known the lad wasn't dead...

Westerly gritted his teeth and bunched his lips together, cursing himself for not checking the boy's pulse thoroughly enough. He'd thought it was too easy…

The young man had been a gift. Young, inexperienced, and totally oblivious to how the world of bloodstock and racing actually operated – he thought sales companies would buy his invention and use it to accurately rate the horses they were selling. As if any auction house would allow such a thing! The balance was purposely tipped significantly in the favour of the vendors, because that's how sales companies made their money!

Westerly ground his teeth until his jaw began to ache. He'd been so unlucky. In his head, his hastily arranged plan had been faultless. Saul Cunningham had been *perfect*. There had been only one element of the plan that required a slice of good luck – he'd had to rely on Porter to lose his temper. The old man had done so... far too thoroughly as it happened, but not thoroughly enough – a bit like the way he'd run the company. Westerly scowled inwardly. He should have smashed the boy's head against the wall himself a few times, just for good measure...

He'd been waiting for the right moment to expose Porter's sudden descent into dementia, as he'd recognised the tell-tale signs several months ago. Just like his boss, Westerly's father had succumbed to dementia in his fifties. He'd lived through this before. The impaired judgement, the slide into moments of fantasy, and worse, when the sufferer wasn't handled properly, the sudden, unexpected trigger that brought about a violent act... That propensity to lash out had been present in Porter, and ever stronger in the last few days, bubbling under the surface as the once great leader of a major racehorse sales house unknowingly descended deeper and deeper into a deluded confusion.

Westerly had swiftly realised what Saul's work could do. The lad had initially called on him a fortnight ago. The value of his innovation was... limitless. Imagine being the only person on the planet who could know the true ability of any racehorse before they raced, and combine that with being the Managing Director of one of the biggest bloodstock sales companies – with unfettered access to a huge number of unraced racehorses... The possibilities were endless. Whoever patented the system could corner the global market in racehorse sales.

On the other hand, making the technology available as Saul had wanted... It would have shaken the foundations of racing to its very core. Bloodstock agents would become superfluous, stud farms without mares with the speed gene would fail, and sales companies... well, virtually all their profit came from selling the *potential* of a racehorse. Who would buy any racehorse that after a two minute scan could be ruled out of *ever* winning a race of any sort? Saul had needed to be stopped…. Or even better, *handled to his own advantage.*

The answer had come to Westerly at the recent yearling sale. Porter was becoming more cantankerous and unpredictable as each day went by, steadily slipping into the grasping hands of his dementia. Westerly's own assent to Managing Director was assured, it was just a matter of timing it for maximum gain. He'd managed to guide Porter through the five day sale without arousing too much suspicion, but, when a prominent buyer had noticed the Managing Directors' increasingly strange behaviour and out of genuine worry enquired whether a visit to the doctor might be in order, Porter had reacted with a flash of violence, aiming a weak fist at the buyer's chin.

It had been a spike of hatred driven by only the smallest suggestion Porter wasn't capable of doing his job... Westerly was sure that somewhere in his head, Porter knew something was amiss, but he was a stubborn and old-fashioned type… and was fighting it, fighting the growing realization he was unwell. Westerly had hurriedly pacified the buyer, whisking Porter away. It was then that he understood his path to potential success… It would hasten his promotion to Managing Director and would solve the problem of Saul Cunningham. He would introduce Saul to Porter and wait… for the inevitable to happen.

During Westerly's first meeting with Saul, the lad had proudly told him he'd worked on gene identification at university, and specifically, the string of gene markers that identified the predisposition to a range of conditions, including dementia. The lad was also principled, there was no way he wouldn't recognise Porter's ailment and not do something about it… like *telling* the old man.

When the argument started, as it surely must do, Westerly planned to enter the scene, quickly dispatch Saul with a letter knife he'd stolen from Porter's office, and blame the old man. Who would the police believe? A totally sane businessman like himself, or a rambling old man with early onset dementia who had swung a very public punch at a client only a few days earlier?

Westerly had cheered inwardly when Porter took the lad to the stables – he'd been expecting to do the deed in the Managing Director's office. He'd planned to pull the blinds down and calm the argument before hitting the lad over the head with one of Porter's awards… Westerly had quite liked that idea. The old man never shut up about his awards. But a quiet stable, away from prying eyes was so much better.

So he'd tracked the two of them to the stable, and waited until voices were raised. Taking a deep breath he'd entered, ready to do the deed with a handy mucking out fork he'd found leaning up against a nearby stable… but once he'd managed to push Porter away from the stable door, he'd discovered the dirty part of his job had already been completed. Only, it hadn't.

Westerly watched with growing dread as Saul Cunningham turned his head on his trolley and said something to one of the ambulance crew. The woman bent over, nodded, then crossed over to a nearby plain clothed policeman. He in turn approached Saul, listened to him, and disappeared into the stable. He emerged a minute later, shaking his head and a further conversation with the lad ensued.

Westerly's mouth went dry as the policeman stepped a pace away from the lad's trolley and half-turned. Saul slowly lifted his arm from his bed, extended a finger, and pointed up at Westerly's window.

The policeman and the ambulance crew turned and shading their eyes, stared up at the small group filling the window. Westerly didn't move, rooted to the spot. He'd stolen the boys laptop and other sensing equipment. It wouldn't take long for the police to find them if they conducted a search.

Thinking furiously, westerly decided he'd have to hand over what he'd stolen. He'd simply tell the police he'd moved them for safe-keeping, having known how important they were to the young man... intending to hand them back.

It would surely take a huge mental leap to suspect he was corrupt enough to use a sick man as a weapon... Westerly tried hard not to grimace as he tracked the police officer's progress towards his office building.

Making his way back to the Managing Director's office, Westerly tried to get comfortable in Porter's executive chair, but found it impossible. As he waited for the policeman's inevitable knock on the glass door, Westerly tried desperately to think of suitable comments he could make, but found himself fixating on the image of the handcuffed Porter climbing into the policeman's car.

What sort of person could even consider him to be *that* corrupt? Westerly thought, his confidence growing. It would take someone with a razor sharp mind and a deeply cynical view of the bloodstock business to even begin to suspect he was involved in the attack on Cunningham.

A knock on the glass door announced the arrival of the plain-clothed policeman. He entered without waiting for permission and asked whether he'd found Mr John Westerly. When he assured him he had, they shook hands and a badge was flashed. Westerly stared at the detective, wondering just how *sharp* he could be. The policeman was examining his hand, the one he'd shaken.

'Anything the matter?' queried Westerly, genuinely confused.

The policeman splayed his fingers and waggled them dexterously, 'No. it's nothing Mr Westerly. I'm just a little surprised.'

'Surprised? At my handshake?'

'I must explain,' replied the detective, 'I own a couple of small shares in racehorses, one of which we bought at your yearling sales.'

Westerly felt queasy. It felt like ice now flowed through his veins.

'My trainer warned me numerous times,' continued the policeman, 'that should I ever shake the hand of a Bloodstock Auction Director, I must always count my fingers afterwards.'

Westerly blinked nervously, unable to conjure up a reply. The policeman seemed to be serious, he was regarding him steadily without any show of emotion. But he couldn't know, he just *couldn't*.

'Tell me Mr Westerly, how long have you known that Mr Porter was suffering from dementia?'

Westerly swallowed hard and tried to ignore the rivulets of perspiration pouring from his forehead. For the first time since sitting down in front of him, the policeman slowly broke into a knowing smile.

A Diabolical Coup

Using his intimidatory skills, Charlie Madden had so far been successful in dominating the four-seater table in the centre of his railway carriage. Noticing it was becoming busier as the train's departure time approached, he renewed his efforts to scowl at any traveller who showed even the slightest inclination to join him.

A well-dressed man pulling a small wheeled suitcase paused and eyed the three empty seats hopefully as he approached. However, when his gaze fell upon Charlie's craggy face, hard stare, and curled lip he quickly averted his eyes and carried on down the carriage. Charlie allowed himself a sly smile once the potential interloper had bundled swiftly past.

The seats remained vacant as the East Coast train jerked to a start and left Kings Cross at 6.43am, on its way to Edinburgh via York. Charlie spread his thin frame as best he could over two seats and more importantly, unfolded today's copy of the Racing Post and laid it across the entire tabletop with a satisfied sigh. As the train entered the tunnel just outside the station, he ran a hand through his short, black dyed hair and settled into his seat to analyse the form for a particularly tricky two mile handicap.

It was Charlie's favourite day of racing; the first day of the Ebor meeting at York. The Great Voltigeur, the Juddmonte, and the Acomb Stakes – it really was a fantastic day of racing and so much more enjoyable than Ebor Day itself, which he felt had become overpopulated with youngsters more interested in getting hopelessly drunk than enjoying the top quality racehorses on show. He hadn't missed this Wednesday up in Yorkshire for twenty years.

He worked hard, and this was one of only a few regular indulgences he allowed himself each year. Now he was reaching his late fifties, he was less likely to be recognised, and even less so on public transport, so could travel to York with the minimum of risk. To the world at large Charlie was the Managing Director of Madden Logistics; his calling card announced this in large, gold embossed capitals and was proffered to people who were impressed by that sort of thing. However, to the few individuals who needed to know, Charlie was a thief.

'I guess this seat isn't taken?'

Charlie had been bent over the small plastic table, concentrating on the form of the fiendishly difficult handicap. He sighed, looked up, and turned his nose up at the young man enquiring after the window seat. Unfortunately, his contemptuous expression was wasted. Looking young enough to be a teenager, the lad had already plonked himself into the seat opposite and was busy pawing through the contents of a white canvass zip-up sports bag with a large gaudy logo on its side.

'If I were you, kid, I'd find somewhere else to sit,' Charlie advised with a growl, 'I'm kinda busy here.'

'Yeah, I saw that. You going racing?' he asked without looking up.

'Seriously, kid. I need the space. Find another seat.'

The lad stopped rummaging around in his bag and placed a sandwich in a triangular box on the table, countering Charlie's steely stare with a hurt expression.

'Aw, cumon. I saw your racing paper,' he said, nodding at the Racing Post open on the plastic topped table, 'I'm going to York races today. Isn't that where you're going?'

'Yes, but I...'

'It's my first time at the races,' the lad interrupted, bouncing slightly in his seat and grinning, apparently from undisguised excitement. His foot poked Charlie's shin under the table as he made himself comfortable. Charlie ground his teeth, making his cheek muscles ripple. The lad didn't appear to notice.

'I don't know what to expect. Never gone horseracing

before. I guess you've been a few times? It would be good if you could give me a few pointers as…'

A redheaded woman in a short tartan pencil skirt and flowery white blouse was suddenly bearing down on the lad with a train ticket in her hand. She was checking the seat numbers.

'I believe I'm sitting here,' she barked at the lad.

'Really?' he replied, his mouth full of bacon sandwich, 'I think *I'm* sitting here, in fact, I'm sure I am.'

The woman gave the lad a withering stare for a second, then transferred her attention to Charlie.'

Charlie shrugged and looked out of the window, giving the impression neither he nor the lad were about to get up.

The woman was clearly irritated, but looked about and seeing that there was a huge selection of free seats, she seemed to decide it wasn't worth making a fuss. She bore down on the lad, thrusting a pointed finger with a sharp red nail towards him so it came within inches of his face.

'Taking a reserved seat for yourself is tantamount to stealing, you know!' she snorted and turned on her heel.

Once the woman had disappeared down the carriage, the lad soon resumed his chatter about York races. Charlie leaned back in his seat, only half-listening. He regarded the lad for a long moment, studying him, weighing him up. It was a valuable skill he'd honed over the years; the ability to analyse every microscopic muscle twitch in a face, understand body language, gestures, and other subtle signs. It was invaluable to be able to read these little 'tells' in strangers. In a matter of a few minutes, Charlie would instinctively know what drove them, their strengths, their weaknesses, their loyalties, and perhaps most importantly, their propensity to tell the truth. The key was to watch what they were saying and not to listen to what they were saying. He'd found it especially useful when associating with criminals. As a rule, Charlie never trusted anyone.

He estimated the lad was aged between eighteen and

twenty-two. He was darkly good looking, in a wiry, shabby sort of way, and wore his tight-fitting moderately expensive suit without a tie and with a unbuttoned grey shirt. He had clean, but not manicured fingernails and his hands looked soft. No tattoos, piercings, jewellery, so it was unlikely he was a gang member; his accent and choice of language backed this up. Yes, this lad had enjoyed a decent, possibly sheltered life to date, and as a result, he knew nothing of the real world. Charlie noted that the lad's face was unmemorable, except for his right-hand eyebrow that had a diagonal gap in its centre, splitting it neatly in two. He'd noticed it as soon as he sat down. It made the kid look like he was permanently quizzical.

'...and my boss at work had this pre-paid ticket and told me to get the first train out of London to York in the morning, so here I am!'

Charlie was decided: the lad was nothing more than a daft youngster out on what was probably his first big adventure alone. He was refreshingly trusting of the people around him, and this made him vulnerable. Charlie smiled inwardly, perhaps he could have some fun with the lad. He'd already chosen most of his selections for the days racing, apart from that twenty-four runner long-distance handicap that would be a nightmare to try and analyse, and besides, the young lad reminded him a little of himself at that age. He could probably do with being toughened up, being taught a few lessons by a grizzled player of the game.

'If you're staying here, move over one seat. At least that way we both get some leg room,' Charlie said brusquely, indicating the aisle seat, 'What's your name, son?'

'Dillon,' the lad answered with a perfectly symmetrical grin, shifting seats and carefully placing his bag on the window seat.

'You say your boss has sent you to York races. What business is he in?'

'I started in Canary Wharf about four months ago. I work for Aidan Brampton, he's a fund manager for Delaney, you know, the pension people? They have those ads on telly with the talking dog. I guess I'm sort of his apprentice. So how long will it take to get to York? I've never been north of Nottingham…'

By the time they had reached their first station stop at Peterborough, Charlie had shared his first name, his job title, the fact he was a seasoned punter at York, and precious little else. Meanwhile, he was now privy to Dillon Dixon's life story from birth. He grew up in Sevenoaks, and as Charlie had suspected, Dillon had enjoyed a privileged upbringing. He'd attended the local primary before moving to a private school, onto university to study economics and then straight into a job in the city at twenty-one, on the first rung of the corporate ladder in financial services. He had a nineteen-year-old girlfriend called Charlotte who was a hair stylist in Canada Square, still went home at weekends (mainly, it seemed, for his beloved mother's Sunday lunch) and supported Arsenal.

Charlie soon discovered Dillon was a shade self-obsessed, driven by money, had a tendency to exaggeration, constantly sought assurance from his listener, and possessed a rose-tinted view of life. However, Charlie could locate no malice, dark edge, or hidden agenda in the lad; he was in the main, truthful. He drove a five-year-old VW Polo GTI, lived in a shared house, loved pizza, hated curry; he'd never fallen in love…

Dillon continued to relate this information at a relentless pace, most of which Charlie allowed to drift over him like soap bubbles, admiring them for a moment before they popped and were forgotten. However, the lad ended with a comparatively interesting story of how close he'd come to death; Dillon was a Type One Diabetic.

To his surprise, Charlie found himself amused by the lad's account of how he'd suffered a hypo when on a motorbike camping holiday with friends. He'd woken fleetingly from his diabetic coma to find himself on the back of a speeding motorbike, having been literally tethered to the rider – the only way his friends could get him safely to hospital and the injection of glucagon essential to save him from drifting even further into a diabetic coma. The lad proudly lifted his suit jacket up to show off an insulin pump he'd started to use only a few weeks earlier, proclaiming it to be '…the best thing since Pot Noodle!'

By the time the train had reached Retford Charlie had begun to feel he had learned everything necessary from the lad. In fact, he was becoming irritated by his travelling companion's ceaseless small talk. He'd decided he would cut the lad loose. That was, until the lad mentioned the bet.

'Run that by me again?'

'That's why I'm going to York,' Dillon explained happily, 'I have to put this bet on a horse for Aidan, my boss. It's a sort of trust thing I think, combined with an initiative test. It's a bit frightening really, I've never placed a bet at a racecourse, but I suppose it can't be that difficult. I've googled it, and placing a bet with an on-course bookie seems straightforward. That said, I will have to…'

'What sort of bet?' Charlie cut in abruptly. Depending on Dillon's reply, he was ready to tell this lad with verbal diarrhoea to jog on and find another seat.

The lad paused for a moment. It was the first time in the entire first hour of their journey that he'd left more than a short breath between sentences.

'I'm not supposed to tell anyone,' he admitted, pursing his lips and scrunching his face up apologetically.

'Oh right. Well, that's okay. I understand,' Charlie said with a shrug. He cast his gaze out of the window, although his concentration wasn't on the flat Lincolnshire countryside currently whizzing past under a stubbornly cloudy morning sky, 'As long as you know what you're doing.'

He watched the lad's reflection in the train window, remaining silent, enjoying the change in expression on Dillon's face as he fought the urge to share his big secret with his new found friend. It was just a matter of time…

'I don't suppose it would hurt,' Dillon ventured five seconds later.

'No, if it's a secret, you know, *a coup*, then there's no need to say anything. I assume this boss of yours... Aidan isn't it? I guess he's given you very specific instructions?'

The lad's eyes widened, 'A coup?'

Charlie turned back to the lad feigning surprise, 'You know, a racing coup... surely you'll have heard about them.'

Dillon swallowed hard. He glanced around the carriage, then surreptitiously leaned over the table.

'You know, it did sound a bit fishy when Aidan told me what was going to happen,' he said in a conspiratorial whisper.

Charlie's brow furrowed and he remained silent.

'I've got to wait for a text message, and then place all of this on the horse,' Dillon said, patting his sports bag.

'All of what?'

Dillon bit his lip and furtively checked the central corridor both ways. Their part of the carriage was empty apart from a woman tapping on her laptop two rows away. He glanced at her then carefully unzipped his sports bag and opened it up on the seat beside him.

'All of this!' he whispered excitedly, pointing a finger encouragingly into the canvas bag.

Charlie gave the lad a sceptical half-smile, leaned over the table and peered into the bag. His smile soon hardened. Underneath a bottle of Lucozade, a Snickers bar, and a packet of salt and vinegar crisps lay a solid bed of flat, pristine, bank-wrapped bundles of fifty pounds notes. From experience, Charlie could tell they were one thousand pound bundles and estimated there was between twenty-five and thirty of them. At that moment the sun broke from behind the clouds and without warning the side of the train was bathed in glorious sunshine. For a second it seemed to Charlie that the notes shimmered with a warm, rosy glow.

Dillon gazed over at the older man expectantly, whilst

running the zip back across the length of the bag until it was resealed. The satisfying tinny rasp from the zip called to Charlie as he pushed back into his seat. The smell of opportunity was now hanging in the air, and what he did and said in the next few minutes would determine whether he could grasp it, or allow it to slip through his fingers. The lad watched him intently, the reflection of the morning sun from the train window making his eyes sparkle.

'Well, what do you think?' the lad asked, unable to keep the excitement from his voice.

Charlie placed his elbows on the table, brought his palms together as if about to pray, and began to bounce his index fingers off his lips. He stared down at the table, as if in deep thought, but in fact he was waiting for the lad to ask his question again. He didn't have to wait long, the lad's impatience saw to that.

'So, *what do you think*? Dillon demanded.

Charlie flicked his eyes up and emitted a long sigh.

'That's a *very* large bet.'

'I know! My boss gave me thirty-thousand pounds.'

Charlie raised both his eyebrows and told the lad, 'It's *too* large.'

'Too large? How can it be too large?'

Charlie gave the lad a wry smile, careful not to come over as condescending or smug.

'You've been handed a difficult, almost impossible task. There's not many on-course bookmakers that will want to lay a thirty-thousand pounds bet from a young chap they've never seen before.'

'I'd have thought they'd jump at it.'

Charlie shook his head, 'There's all sorts of things you have to consider. If you think you can just walk up to the first bookie you come across, tell him the horse's name, empty thirty thousand pounds into his satchel and he'll just smile and give you a betting ticket, then think again.'

For the first time that morning, the lad was speechless.

His mouth opened and closed twice and his brow creased with concern.

'What does... I mean, how... Uhhh! How am I going to back the horse I'm given?' he eventually managed.

Charlie gave the sports bag a sceptical stare, then checked his watch before locking eyes with his young travelling companion.

'I guess we've got what remains of this journey to get you up to speed.'

***

Charlie had always been possessed of a sharp, agile mind, and combined with a total lack of empathy, he was not only adept at parting fools from their money, but could do so without feeling anything for his many victims. That said, he chose his victims very carefully indeed. By the time the train pulled away from Doncaster station he had the young lad convinced that he needed Charlie by his side. His best chance was to utilise Charlie's deep knowledge of racing, and allow the older man to guide him through the afternoon.

'There are many different factors in play, each one could affect your ability to get your money on at the longest odds,' he explained to Dillon, 'I imagine you are just one cog in a much bigger and complex machine. The reason the name of the horse is being sent to you at a specific time is because whoever is orchestrating this coup doesn't want the price of the horse to crash before they get all their money on at the longest odds possible.'

Charlie explained that as Dillon was expecting to receive his text message with the horse's name at 4-00pm, it must be running in the 4-10pm at York, as his instructions were to place his bet as soon as he was given the name of the racehorse. The exchanges, online bookmakers, and the course bookmakers would all be hit with large bets for the same horse at the same time. Each bookmaker would hopefully accept the bets at the current odds, unaware that they would be unable to lay-off at a similar or higher price, as the horse's odds would tumble everywhere almost immediately. The key to the coup was the timing of the bets. He asked Dillon if he knew of any other people like him being involved, but wasn't surprised when the lad gave him a blank stare in return.

Referring to his Racing Post, Charlie remarked, 'The 4-10pm is a highly competitive two mile handicap with over twenty runners. The favourite is five to one, so your boss, or whoever is running the coup, must be looking for a huge payday.'

Once again, Dillon returned him an apologetic shrug. Charlie noticed the lad's bravado and childish enthusiasm for the task had evaporated. He was looking small and vulnerable, and he was picking nervously with finger and thumb at the zip on the sports bag.

'Never mind, son. Stick with me and we'll make sure you get that money on at decent odds. Your boss will be giving you a raise and a promotion once this task has been completed successfully,' Charlie assured the lad with a well-practiced fatherly smile.

Having never had children, or even a wife for that matter, Charlie couldn't be absolutely sure it was a fatherly smile. However, he'd duped plenty of people with that same reassuringly honest and friendly expression. It transmitted peace of mind and removed doubt. His mark would often come alive as he transferred his own confidence into them, emptying all but the most ingrained second thoughts from their heads. Even now, in his late fifties, he regularly worked on that smile in front of the mirror. That smile was responsible for a number of his biggest scores.

Dillon immediately brightened. He sat up in his seat and with renewed vigour asked, 'You'll be there with me?'

'Sure. We need to split up and place the bets in five thousand pound chunks, the bookies are far more likely to accept that sort of stake. That's three bets each, and we'll time it so we both hit the rails together.'

The lad's frown returned and Charlie swiftly plastered his reassuring smile back onto his face, 'The *rails bookmakers*. They're the big lads. The sort of bookies that won't recoil when they see bundles of money like yours.'

'How will I know who they are?' Dillon queried, 'Are they on those white rails beside the racetrack.'

Charlie almost laughed out loud. This lad was as green as grass.

'No. Don't worry, I'll point out the three bookmakers you need to approach well before the race. And as you place your bets, I'll be only a few yards to your right, placing the other bets along the line of rails bookmakers. We'll meet up after we've each placed our three bets at good, long odds.'

The train trundled into York station just after nine o'clock and Charlie guided Dillon over the footbridge and together they made their way through the architecturally impressive station building and out into the sunshine, the early morning cloud having slipped away. Across the road, the stone of the city walls shone white in the sunlight, brilliantly offset by the green grass that sloped up to meet its base. Charlie sucked in a deep breath of fresh air and turned to Dillon.

'Breakfast?'

The lad's eyes lit up, 'Sure, Charlie.'

The two of them set off walking towards the city and Charlie stole a glance at the lad. Dillon was striding along, full of the innocence and confidence of youth, his eyes darting everywhere and a constantly astonished smile on his face. Charlie wondered what the lad was thinking, and began to smile himself. He got the impression the lad was feeling like they were two gunslingers, all set to cause a rumpus in this small, northern city.

Charlie's timetable for his trip to York races always included breakfast. He would book a table at a reassuringly upmarket café located beside the River Ouse and enjoy watching the pleasure boats drift past as he tucked into his full English breakfast served by attentive and professional waitresses. This was followed by a gentle thirty to forty minute stroll to the racecourse that helped settle the meal.

As they crossed under the city wall and over Lendal Bridge Charlie reflected that it was a shame he was having to reveal one of his favourite haunts to Dillon, but it was important to keep the lad, and his money, as close as possible throughout the day.

As they ate, Charlie explained odds to his young charge, and the importance of reading the text message fully once it arrived at four o'clock – just in case the instructions would be to place their bets each-way, rather than just a straight win. He warned Dillon to ask the bookmakers for a price and ensure each betting ticket reflected the odds he had asked for, he told him to check each bundle of cash before they reached the racecourse, and advised him to place bets with the same rails bookmakers in the earlier races to help make himself known to them. He also told him to eat the crisps, as if the horse won, he'd need plenty of room in his bag.

The lad seemed to be transfixed with every word that slipped from his mouth, avidly taking on board every scrap of advice, checking he understood, and asking questions.

'Would you mind if I backed the horse with a little of my own money?' Charlie asked as he placed a ten pounds tip beneath his coffee cup, having insisted he pay for the meal.

Dillon gave this a few seconds thought, 'I don't suppose it will matter, will it?'

'No, I usually bet in fifty pounds stakes, but it would be nice to have a few hundred on, just to be part of the coup. An extra few hundred quid added to the last five thousand pounds bets I place for you won't affect anything...'

'It's the least I can do, given how much help you've given me. I really don't know how I'd have managed without you, Charlie. You've been an absolute godsend.'

The lad's words instilled no pride, or guilt in Charlie. Neither did he pity Dillon. He felt nothing, he was doing his job.

'Good. I'll need to go into the city and visit the bank to get the cash, but we've got plenty of time. The first race isn't until ten to two.'

The two men walked together at an easy pace, Charlie slowing every now and again to peer into a shop window, or point out a piece of old-world architecture to Dillon. Passing countless pubs and cafes, Charlie paused outside a large music shop displaying a range of keyboards, guitars, and numerous other instruments, sheet music, and 'how to play' books in the window display.

'Won't be a minute,' he told the younger man and disappeared inside, emerging two minutes later with a small, oblong bulge in his blazer pocket.

'A present for a friend,' he explained, tapping the lump.

Charlie was a full ten minutes inside the bank on Parliament Street, having had to visit the human teller on the second floor to receive his cash, rather than using an automated machine. As he returned to the ground floor he noticed Dillon outside on the pavement, having an animated conversation on his mobile phone. The call was quickly curtailed when he stepped outside the bank, with Dillon greeting him with a plastic smile.

'Everything okay?'

'Yes,' Dillon confirmed with an exaggerated sigh, 'Just my Mother, worrying about me!'

Charlie nodded his understanding and wasted no time setting off for the racecourse.

***

York Racecourse's grandstand loomed large in front of them as they approached down the long, straight, tree-lined boulevard to the east of the course. The path was thronged with people and a steady flow of cars to their left was filling the grassed centre of the Knavesmire, line by line. As they drew closer, Charlie was witness to an alteration in Dillon's disposition. From overly chatty, the lad suddenly became silent, brimming full of nervous anticipation.

'You said this was your first time at York races?'

'My first time at any racecourse,' he replied after a pause.

They entered the County Stand enclosure through separate gates, Dillon waiting in line with his pre-paid ticket while Charlie produced several notes from his wallet, entered quickly, and was waiting inside the course when the lad finally emerged from the gate looking flustered.

Dillon spied Charlie and hurried over, 'The security guy insisted on looking inside my bag.'

Charlie returned a crooked half-smile, 'And…?'

'He gave me this funny look, and said, 'The very best of luck to you, sir,' and waved me through.'

'What did you expect? The course will be hoping you place your bets through the Tote. They get up to thirty percent cut on every bet placed, They're hardly going to stop you bringing in a wad of money.'

'But I've got thirty thousand pounds in cash!'

'Keep your voice down,' Charlie warned in a whispered hiss, 'There are always pickpockets at this meeting, looking out for an easy touch. Besides, if your boss's inside information is good, imagine what you'll have in your bag when you *leave* the course!'

Once his words had registered with Dillon the lad fell silent, his eyes darting suspiciously around people in the local vicinity. Charlie lightly clapped a reassuring hand to the lad's shoulder and his look of bewilderment slowly faded from his young face.

'Come on, my valiant young gambler,' Charlie said, his words imbued with amusement, 'Let me introduce you to the County Stand Enclosure of York Racecourse. Let's get you suitably acquainted with the lay of the land.'

By the time the first race of the day, a valuable sprint handicap, had gone off at ten minutes to two, Charlie had toured Dillon around every building in the Premier enclosure. He'd introduced him to the rails bookmakers and together they had divided up which of the colourful and imposing figures, both men and women, they would approach with their bets when the all-important text message arrived and the two of them would enter the bear pit, each attempting to strike three bets of five thousand pounds at the best prices available.

At quarter to four Charlie looked over at Dillon and studied the lad. They were leaning against a steel rail, a little way up the grandstand steps, overlooking the rails betting area. The lad looked distinctly queasy. He'd lost his glow of excitement and although he was watching the horses cantering to post for the 4:10pm race, Charlie doubted he was really aware of what was going on. Dillon had his mobile phone lying on his palm and was checking it every few seconds, tapping at the screen whenever it faded to black.

When big, fat beads of sweat started to burst from his forehead, Charlie placed a steadying hand on the lad's arm and asked whether he was okay. Dillon nodded back and attempted a smile, assuring him it was simply nerves. Charlie noticed Dillon's right hand was grinding away at the nylon handles of the sports bag. It was a fine, summers day, perfect weather for flat racing, but the drips of sweat running down Dillon's fist signalled all was not as it should be. Charlie wondered whether he should act, but instead, he waited. He waited, and watched as the colour drained from the young man's face.

The grandstand was starting to fill with racegoers for the ten past four race and Charlie suggested they move down to ground level to wait for the all-important text message. Dillon nodded his silent agreement. His stomach was leaning against the rail, his left hand gripping it and with the other he held the sports bag. He pushed away from the steel bar and said, 'Just a sec, I'm going to have a bite of something.'

It was three minutes to four-o'clock when Dillon bent down, and with trembling hands, unzipped his sports bag, took out the chocolate bar and straightened. He'd only just managed to rip the wrapper off and sink his teeth into his Snickers when his eyelids fluttered, his knees buckled, and he dropped with wild, flailing arms, trying to clutch any object that would keep him upright. Three fingers of one sweaty hand gained a grip on Charlie's blazer. Charlie soon came to the lad's aid, slinging an arm around his waist and guiding Dillon to a seated position on the steps. Thankfully, the lad was surprisingly light, however he tipped over and lay sideways on the step.

'Dillon! What's the matter?' Charlie asked urgently.

The lad's eyes rolled and momentarily flicked inhumanly in their sockets.

'I'm… going hypo… glycaemic,' the lad stammered, still gripping the sports bag handles, drawing it tightly to his chest, '… the Lucozade…'

Charlie fiddled with the zip of the sports bag and recovered the small plastic bottle of amber liquid from within. Wrenching the top off, he guided it onto Dillon's lips. He leaned the lad's head back and began to tip small, regular amounts of sugar-rich Lucozade over his tongue, pausing the flow if the lad gurgled or coughed.

Barely a quarter of the small bottle had entered the lad's lips when two loud electronic beeps sounded close by. A small group of racegoers had turned and created a small arc on the steps of the stands around them, and a middle-aged lady now stepped up and proffered Dillon's phone to Charlie.

'This must be his. He must have dropped it when he…'

Charlie thanked the woman and taking it from her, read the message on the illuminated screen. It read, 'Diabolical to win, 4-10pm York.'

Charlie looked down at Dillon, still on his side and now

taking short, sharp breaths. Some semblance of colour was returning to his face and Charlie knelt down and pushed him into a seated position.

Charlie started, 'The text message…'

'You have to place the bets…' Dillon cut in, managing a longer, deeper breath and finishing with a grimace, 'I'll need more… time.'

Charlie opened his mouth to reply, but the lad shook his head and weakly pulled Charlie close to him, 'Just… go… I trust you,' and pushed a weak palm against Charlie's chest, releasing the sports bag at the same time.

He didn't argue. Charlie took the bag, tapped the lad's shoulder and said, 'Don't worry, I'll be back in a minute,' and disappeared from the lad's view.

It was three minutes past four by the time Charlie fought he way through the massing crowd, reached the bottom of the grandstand, and was standing on the fringes of the betting concourse. In front of him lines of bookmakers were doing a brisk trade in a race that boasted a long priced favourite that showed at 9/2 and 5/1 in a place. He ran his eyes down the electronic boards and located Diabolical and his heart missed a beat when he read 25/1 in glowing orange light to the right of the gelding's name. Charlie checked another board, and another… each offered 25/1, a fourth advertised 33/1.

Ignoring the urge to look back up the stand steps to where Dillon would be sitting, slowly recovering from his diabetic hypo, Charlie moved forward, sidestepping punters, his eyes on the prize; the 33/1 offered on the fourth board. Several options were competing for dominance in his mind, each of them would see him leave the racecourse many thousands of pounds wealthier, but he ignored their urgent calling to him, keeping his eyes on the biggest prize of all.

Charlie approached the bookmaker, waited until a bet of £20 on the favourite had been recorded to the chap in front of him and took a breath before telling the expectant bookie who already had his hand held out to receive his cash, 'Lay me ten grand to win at 33's on Diabolical, number seventeen.'

The bookie blinked and dropped his hand, assessing Charlie from head to foot. His analysis complete, he turned to his associate and had a short whispered conversation, returning to Charlie to ask, 'Cash?' The query was answered by Charlie immediately, as he opened the sports bag and flashed the stacks of fifty pounds notes.

'You can have five at 33's and the rest at SP,' the bookie offered.

'No Starting Price, give me the other five at 25/1,' Charlie countered.

A wry smile crept onto the bookie's face and he nodded his agreement. Charlie grabbed ten bundles of a thousand pounds from the bag and tipped them into the bookies open bag and two separate betting tickets spewed forth from the small printing machine attached to his stand. The bookie tore them off and handed them over to Charlie adding, 'Thanks for your business, Mr…?'

'Madden,' said a sarcastic voice from over Charlie's shoulder, 'Charlie Madden.'

The bookie frowned at the two gentlemen behind his newest customer and his lip curled as an arm extended and a Metropolitan Policeman's badge was thrust his way. Charlie hadn't moved, he experienced the entire conversation through the bookie's reactions, which had now turned to disgruntlement.

A heavy hand landed on his shoulder and the same voice announced, 'Charlie Madden, we'd like to speak with you in connection with an attempt to launder the proceeds of criminal activity…'

As the policeman spoke, Charlie slowly spun around and smiled warmly at the two plain clothed gentlemen. He waited until the older of the two officers had added, 'Void that bet mate, and hand over the cash,' upon which Charlie's smile broadened and he said, 'Hello there, Officers. Is Brian with you?'

As Charlie was escorted by the arms through the crowd by the two plain clothes detectives he looked up into the area of the stand where Dillon had been sitting recovering. It was a sea of faces, and yet he was sure he spotted a young man with a pale complexion and a gap over his right eyebrow follow his progress into the bowels of the grandstand. He also could have sworn the lad's face was now full of righteous indignation.

***

Having been marched through a tunnel beneath the County Stand, Charlie was led to a small building that housed the Princess Mary Seafood Bar, and once behind the serving area, he was deposited in a small, windowless ante-room containing a pub picnic bench and precious little else. He was instructed to sit down. Charlie sniffed, and received a sharp waft of prawn dressing up his nose as one of the detectives left the room. Despite the bench being uncomfortable he forced a wan smile onto his lips and patiently crossed his legs.

Almost immediately the detective returned with a portly man in an ill-fitting high street suit that displayed an inch of his sock. He bowled into the room with a broad smile on his doughy face. The door was closed and the two detectives edged back against the wall.

'Brian!' Charlie exclaimed in melodramatic delight before the man could speak, 'I was *hoping* it would be you... and I haven't been disappointed... It *is* you!'

Brian Love's smile flattened somewhat when he realised there was nowhere to sit except on a pub bench, but recovered his composure and cocked his leg over the picnic table to place himself opposite his prisoner.

'It's Chief Inspector Love, as you well know, Charlie,' he murmured, 'You know why you've been brought here?'

Charlie compressed his lips and slowly shook his head.

'You've been set up good and proper this time, Charlie. Remember Billy Salman? I'm sure you do - he went down for nine years for his involvement in a series of bank robberies. You know the ones, his outfit ram-raided cash machines beside night clubs and casinos, cutting them out of the walls with specialist equipment before making off with the whole machine. You must remember...'

Charlie thoughtfully tapped an index finger to his lips, 'It rings a distant bell, but perhaps remind me a bit more, would you? I love the way you tell a story, Brian. You really bring the bare facts to life.'

A public address announcement penetrated the small room; the horses were at the start and the stalls loading process for the twenty runners had commenced.

Brian sighed heavily and closed his tired eyes, rubbing his cheeks and eventually massaged his jaw line for a short time. He was weary of this relationship with Madden and wanted it to end. The tip off had almost certainly come from Billy Salman, an entirely loathsome and violent individual who had thoroughly deserved to go to prison. He wasn't proud of acting upon such a source, but if today's jaunt up north allowed him to finally get a charge to stick on Madden, nothing else mattered. Brian could live with the knowledge that he'd effectively aided a criminal like Salman to exact some revenge.

He'd decided on the journey up to York, just in case the tip off was genuine. The twenty year dance between himself and Madden had gone on long enough. Despite being investigated dozens of times in relation to scores of thefts over the years, Madden maintained a pristine police record. He didn't even have a parking offence, due in main to the target of his criminal activities. Madden chose to steal exclusively from businesses with questionable reputations, and run by questionable individuals.

Due to retire in eighteen months' time, Brian had had enough of being the butt of his colleagues jokes. He was cast as the aging policemen who doggedly pursued Madden, but never managed to catch him. He'd also had enough of being humiliated by an annoyingly clever and cocky criminal who only stole from the sort of lowlife's that deserved it. He'd lived with that tag among the police ranks for most of his career, and it had gone on long enough. Brian wanted his last year in the job to be 'Madden-free'.

'Billy Salman reckons you nicked almost half a million quid from him, and when he demanded it back with menaces, you let the Met know, anonymously of course, that the remaining cash machines - the ones he still couldn't successfully open - were in one of his lockups.'

Brian had locked eyes with Charlie half-way through this speech. Charlie didn't flinch, he stared back with a glazed expression, his eyelids only half open, as if further information of this kind might force him to nod off.

'I reckon Billy Salman has been mulling over how to exact his revenge on you for the last five years he's spent in prison,' Brian continued, 'He was released on parole a month ago. And then, would you believe it, we get another anonymous call last night saying that the Robin Hood of thieves, the great untouchable Charlie Madden is going to try to launder thirty thousand pounds from that cash machine robbery at York races today!'

'Gosh, that sounds terribly exciting!' Charlie exclaimed, leaning forward, 'And to cap it all, I've been painted as the kingpin in this dastardly plot…'

Brian's eyes narrowed. He'd been expecting a slightly less exuberant reaction. He eyed the sports bag on the table.

'Let's take a look, shall we?'

As the contents of the white canvass bag were deposited onto the picnic table, a shout of, 'They're off!' echoed around the racecourse. Thirty thousand pounds was quickly counted out, in one-thousand pound paper wrapped bundles, and stacked up neatly by the detective who had escorted Charlie from the rails bookmakers. Finally, the detective dug back into the bag and placed an unwrapped Snickers chocolate bar beside the money, telling his boss that was everything.

'You know we can check the serial numbers of the notes,' Brian said quietly, 'If they match any of the missing money you'll be going to prison for more than five years.'

Charlie cocked his head and concentrated, as Diabolical was mentioned as being prominent in the commentary now coming into the room in waves above the sound of the crowd in the stands and customers next door in the seafood bar.

'Wouldn't it be ironic if Diabolical actually won?' he asked, staring up into the corner of the room and again cocking his ear toward the commentary, 'I might sue the Met...'

Brian's patience ran out. He smacked a flat palm onto the wooden table, making both his detectives jump. Conversely, Charlie slowly turned his head to sullenly regard the Chief Inspector.

'It's taken twenty years, but I've got you now, haven't I?' Brian said with a faintly cruel grin, 'Come on Charlie, admit it. When we check this money…'

'It was sensible not to arrest me,' Charlie interrupted in a serious, deadpan voice, 'Far less embarrassing this way.'

Brian frowned and felt his confidence ebb slightly. He recognised Charlie's tone.

'Take a look at the money,' Charlie continued, 'If it was from a robbery five years ago it would be made of paper, or to be more exact, a type of cloth, and also have a completely different design. This money is made of polymer, and is the new design of fifty pounds with a rather fetching depiction of Alan Turing on the back, I might add.'

Charlie flipped one of the bundles over with his forefinger, 'The old and new notes are still acceptable currency of course, as we're in the change-over period. However, polymer notes weren't around five years ago, so these notes can't be from the cash machine robberies.'

The two detectives on their feet swapped an uneasy glance and Brian stared slack-jawed at the stacks of fifty pound notes in front of him.

'I took this money from my own bank account this morning in the centre of York, intending to have a jolly good bet on a horse I really fancied for a race. The same race that now only has a few furlongs left to run. So if we're done here, gentlemen, I'd really like to see whether the horse you prevented me from backing turns out to be the winner.'

Charlie swung his legs out from under the picnic seat and stood up expectantly. Brian remained seated for a moment, continuing to stare at the money, but he eventually did the same although he was careful not to catch Charlie's eye.

'Give him his money,' he growled at one of the detectives, and stumped out of the room in a waft of shellfish.

The money was quickly tipped back into the sports bag and unceremoniously shoved into Charlie's arms.

'What now?' snarled the detective when Charlie didn't move.

'My Snickers bar,' he said with a pleasant smile, nodding at the table.

***

Charlie entered the restaurant at the Holiday Inn York at seven o-clock and cast his gaze around. A small number of tables were occupied, dotted around the large room, and upon spotting the person he was there to meet, he strode over to her wearing a broad smile. She was taller than Charlie, in her late thirties and wore a striking white flowered blouse and tartan skirt that perfectly offset her long, curling dark red hair.

'Hello, Emily. You're a sight for sore eyes and no mistake,' he said, before planting a dry kiss on his business partner's cheek and joining her at her intimate little table within a booth well away from the other hotel residents.

'And this is for you,' he said with a subtle flash of his eyes, placing a small oblong box in the centre of the table.

Emily smiled uncertainly and upon opening the brightly coloured box discovered a shiny new mouth organ wrapped in cloth.

'I don't know what to say,' she said in a purposefully nonplussed tone.

Charlie stifled a half-laugh, 'I couldn't spot you behind us as we walked into York, so I decided to make the lad wait so you could catch up. That was the only thing in the entire music shop I could find that was small enough to carry!'

'I shall always treasure it, Charlie. Actually, I wasn't too far away, and guessed you'd be heading to the bank. You may not have recognised me, I'd bought some sunglasses and a head scarf while you were treating the lad to the rather nice breakfast that should have been mine.'

'Ah, yes. I'd forgotten about that. The mouth organ doesn't quite make up for ruining your day out does it?'

'Never mind. I still enjoyed it!' Emily said in her low, rich voice, 'What about you, have you recovered yet?'

'Just about. Thank goodness Billy Salman's son didn't recognise you, or at least realise we were travelling together. When you came to take your seat on the train you almost sat on him!'

'Hmm.. yep, sorry,' Emily said with a grimace, 'I only recognised your signal at the very last minute. I know you've been expecting something like this since his father was released from prison, but how did you know who the lad was? You usually give anyone trying to sit with us short shrift.'

Charlie began pouring himself a glass of red wine from a bottle in the centre of the table and winked at Emily as he took his first sip, 'His eyebrow. Billy Salman has the same chunk of his eyebrow missing over his right eye, it must be a genetic thing. At first I wasn't sure, but thought it was worth playing along to find out. If I was trying to frame someone, I'd also choose a day that's always in my target's diary every year. It makes them so much easier to predict.

Anyway, the money in the sports bag confirmed it was a hustle. Billy Salman wouldn't have realised that new polymer fifty pounds notes had been released whilst he was in prison.'

'By the way, great job finding an exact copy of the bag and its contents so quickly after we spoke in the bank, and at such short notice,' Charlie added.

'The lad must have got most of it from Sports Direct. That's where I found it,' Emily said, pausing to sip at her wine, 'It was fairly straightforward.'

'It was important both bags looked and contained exactly the same stuff, just in case anything went wrong. I assumed he'd make sure I was the one to place the bets with the stolen money, I just didn't know how he'd make it happen. I was impressed with him feigning a diabetic hypo. I'm guessing he slipped himself some drug to simulate the signs of low sugar.'

'How did you know it wasn't a real hypo?'

Charlie grinned, 'Dillon must have thought just hooking an insulin pump to his stomach with a medicated patch would be enough to fool me. Apart from the fact it was done so crudely, all those pumps do is release insulin, they don't check the sugar levels in the blood. You still need to monitor your blood and adjust the pump accordingly. He never checked his blood or altered his pump all day, so I knew after a few hours it was just a ruse. Oh, by the way, you know the lad ate the Snickers?'

'Blast, Really? I saw you giving him the Lucozade, and took it out of the duplicate bag with your cash in it, but I must have missed him eating the Snickers.'

Charlie pursed his lips and shook his head, 'He didn't eat it, he took one bite and...'

Emily raised an eyebrow, 'I think you've found the cause of the lad's sudden sweat and paleness. The chocolate bar must have had something in it to bring on the symptoms of low sugar.'

'Well, well,' Charlie said, smarting slightly, 'It must be my age, I missed that completely. I thought Brian and the detectives were working together, and the chocolate and Lucozade might have been signals, you know, a way for Dillon to communicate with the police, letting them know I was about to place the bets.'

'It was all a convoluted plan to allow Dillon to pass you all the dirty money and place the bets,' said Emily.

'To be honest, I'm impressed with the lad's dedication. It had to be his own plan, as his father isn't capable of something that complex. Feigning diabetes was a clever idea, he just executed it poorly.'

Emily nodded, 'So your nemesis, Brian Love, wasn't in league with Dillon, he really did turn up at the races in the hope he'd catch you placing a bet with the cash machine money and charge you with money laundering.'

'Brian must have been tipped off, but it looks that way,' Charlie agreed, 'His reaction when he saw the new fifties was disappointment, not surprise. He mustn't have realised we swapped the bags as I came down the grandstand steps.'

They fell into silence for a minute, refilling their drinks and inspecting the evening menu, both reflecting on the strangeness of their day.

'What are we going to do with the thirty grand in old fifties?' asked Emily as she scanned the starters.

An impish smile crept onto Charlie's face, 'Billy's lad touched the money. His fingerprints will be all over them. That means we hold evidence of his young lad handling stolen money. I'll be writing a very friendly letter to Billy telling him the money will never see the light of day again, as long as he leaves us alone.'

Emily showed her approval with a smile that lit up her face, 'Good stuff! Besides, it would be difficult trying to launder those old fifties.'

'Yeah,' Charlie agreed, 'Billy targeted cash machines outside clubs and casinos, thinking they'd hold more cash. He was right, but he didn't realise those machines are the only ones that actually give out fifties. Trying to launder fifty pounds notes is a nightmare compared to twenties.'

A waiter appeared and they ordered, waiting until he was out of earshot before resuming their conversation.

Emily asked, 'By the way, what happened to that horse, you know, the pretend coup?'

'It was a horse called Diabolical.'

'And…' Emily pressed.

'It led until the final hundred yards, and then got swallowed up by the chasing pack and finished nowhere,' said Charlie with a strangely regretful sigh, 'The commentary had it way out in the lead for most of the race.'

'Why so introspective, Charlie? Diabolical was just a random horse Billy Salman picked to try and fool you.'

Charlie returned Emily a sad smile, 'Yeah, I know. Perhaps I'm going soft as I grow older, but inside that windowless room, half-listening to the race commentary, there was a small part of me that actually wanted Diabolical to win.'

Emily was about to question his logic but immediately thought better of it. Charlie was rarely melancholic; however, as she studied him idly swirling his wine around his glass, she sensed an air of depression had settled upon him. She waited, and presently he spoke again.

'You know, for a moment, one fleeting moment in the grandstand, I was excited about the bet. My heart was pounding and I felt more alive than I've done for ages. I wanted that coup to be real. I really wanted Dillon to be a daft, but above all, an *honest* young lad who was just trying to impress his boss. I wanted to be part of something like that.'

'You're going soft in your old age,' Emily said demurely, flashing him a warm smile.

'Perhaps I am,' Charlie replied sadly, still staring at the

contents of his wine glass. He looks old, Emily thought. Could it be that Charlie Madden, the scourge of The Met, was finished? She studied him for a long moment, unaware of the worry lines slowly deepening across her forehead.

All at once, Charlie's expression altered and his eyes widened. He put his wine glass down and met Emily's gaze. She recognised that look and immediately felt relief wash over her. He'd hit upon a scheme.

'Emily, my dear, maybe we should look into setting up a *proper* racing coup…' said Charlie, suddenly looking twenty years younger, 'Do you know any crooked bookmakers who deserve to have their ill-gotten gains… redistributed?'

The Fall

A mixture of groans and intakes of breath from the crowd greeted the fall.

'…Frampton is down,' exclaimed the race commentator, 'When coming with a promising challenge, he's taken a heavy fall and both horse and jockey are down on the ground.'

Hugo was only dimly aware of the wave of exasperation, shock, and concern mixed with excitement that came from the stands. He lay on the cool, welcoming turf, his chest expanding and contracting as the sound of hooves faded into the distance. Checking himself over, his legs felt okay, and his spine was similarly in working order, despite the fact he had virtually somersaulted before slapping onto the turf after the fence. This was a relief, his back still played up since that fall four years ago; he didn't want months away from the racecourse again.

Getting stiffly to his feet, he became aware he'd not entirely managed to cheat injury. His backside was thumping with pain, no doubt bruised, rather than anything more serious. When he thought about it, he'd been lucky, landing squarely on his rump, instead of his head. He hobbled a few steps and the throbbing slowly dissipated.

He breathed in deeply, filling his lungs successfully. Lifting his head and stretching his neck, expelling the air through his nose, he shivered, and scanned the area around him. A car on the inside of the track drew to a halt and behind it, another vehicle was pulling up. Assistance would be here soon.

But they were of little interest at the moment. Uppermost in his mind was his partner in that disastrous jump at the third last. The object of his search wasn't difficult to find. He lay a little way away from the fence. Despite his stiffness of movement, Hugo was soon bent over the unmoving body. It was a body he knew well. They'd travelled all over the country, won races together, lost races together. They'd run through rain, sleet, snow, and jumped around so many tracks around the North of England, so many chase fences, he couldn't possibly count them.

Looking down at his partner, his friend, Hugo knew those times might be over. Mud-splattered, drawing breath in short, painful gulps, Frampton lay awkwardly, unnaturally. His legs and torso were folded, unmoving, and he was making a disturbing whining. Air rattled in his throat. A wave of acute sadness threatened to smother Hugo; his friend was suffering. The people from the support vehicles were still many yards away, so Hugo bent down and carefully nudged his friend, only as much as he could, but Frampton's breathing was soon much improved.

There was little else he could do for the poor soul, so Hugo started to talk to Frampton.

'Sorry about this, old friend.'

Frampton stared up at Hugo. Large, scared brown eyes blinked, and began to glisten. But the talking helped; his friend's short breaths seemed to lengthen as he relaxed.

'I wanted to put in a big jump at the fence, but didn't reckon on that mare taking our ground,' said Hugo.

Frampton didn't reply. He closed his eyes and waited, glad of the company but fearing what was about to happen to him.

Hugo continued, 'Do you remember that day at Newcastle? The fog was so thick you could hardly see the fences until they were a stride or two in front of you. It was crazy really, when you look back. But then we've done a few crazy things over the last eight years, haven't we?'

Frampton's eyes misted and began to close. Hugo went on, 'We won that day. It was hilarious, no one knew who'd won until we'd walked into the winners enclosure. That reporter from the television came over and asked if we knew who had won the race and didn't believe it was us!'

Frampton blinked, moved his shoulder slightly, and his

eyes lost some of their mistiness; Hugo took it as a good sign.

'Then there was that race at Sedgefield two years ago. The ground was so heavy we were sinking a foot into it with every step,' he said with a smile in his voice, 'We set off on the second circuit in a share of the lead and one by one, the challengers fell away. Talk about atrocious ground! Do you remember, we managed to haul ourselves over the last fence and actually walked the last hundred yards uphill to the finish. We were the only ones to get around the course that day.'

Hugo looked around again. The ambulance and other support staff were running towards them. Bending down once more, Hugo placed his nose close to Frampton's ears.

'It won't be long now,' he whispered, 'Help is coming. This lot will look after you. I'm going to have to leave you soon, but keep your mind full of the good times my old friend. Whatever comes next, remember we had some good times together...'

Frampton's eyes opened, slowly focussed, and swivelled upwards. He could feel his friend's breath wafting onto his cold skin. It was warm and reassuring. His own breath was steady now, he was beginning to feel a tingling, first in his chest and down his back and finally, into his legs.

He was aware of his old friend moving backwards and suddenly there were two, then three, no... five people around him.

'Frampton! Joe! Can you hear me?'

Joe Frampton looked into a concerned face that had bent down level with him, close to the turf. He recognised the racecourse doctor. He tried to move his tongue and reply, but with his face half-pointed into the grass and mud, the effort of trying to speak was too much.

'What's your name?' the doctor demanded.

Willing his mouth to work, he tried again, summoning all his strength and concentration to answer.

'Joe... Frampton, people call me... Frampton.'

'Okay, good. Don't try to move. Just breathe,' the doctor warned.

Frampton settled for the smallest of nods.

'You've been very lucky,' the doctor told Joe busying himself, checking him all over for what felt like an age, and finally placing an oxygen mask over his nose and mouth.

'Both your lungs have almost collapsed. If you hadn't landed in this position you could have asphyxiated before I got here.'

Over the doctor's shoulder, a voice called, 'Wasn't him doc. I was first here. This horse here got up, went over to him and sort of pushed him with his head until he was lying like that.'

The doctor didn't reply, perhaps too busy, or simply believing the man's ridiculous remark didn't warrant a reply.

Frampton blinked, clearing tears that had suddenly swelled into his eyes. He peered underneath, past the doctor's kneeling frame to where the speaker, a man in a green racecourse jacket was standing, holding onto the reins of a familiar bay horse with a wide white blaze running down his nose. The horse was gazing steadily at him. His horse. His ride. His Hugo.

He gave a short cough, and a smile quivered onto his lips under the plastic oxygen mask. Joe Frampton rolled his tongue around his mouth, desperately trying to summon up enough moisture into order to speak.

'Thanks, Hugo,' he croaked.

The doctor plunged a syringe into Frampton's arm and the jockey felt a numbness travel around his body as the painkiller did its work. He was suddenly desperately sleepy.

He was dimly aware of a helicopter ride, being transferred from cradle to bed and into a sterile smelling room, and many faces, many people doing things to him and for him. But all this time Joe Frampton, amateur jockey, didn't fret, he didn't worry. From deep down, Frampton remembered some advice; he relaxed, and allowed his mind to wander as the doctors began the job of putting him back together. The races came to him in extraordinary detail, carried within ripples of memory, delivered in a soft, warm dreamscape.

Each recollection filled him with pleasure. Mounted on Hugo, the two of them as one, Frampton remembered the good times.

Turning Professional

After receiving and returning a familiar wave from the steward in the racecourse carpark, Danny Vickers trundled over the bumpy grass and parked his tiny Fiat. His was one of the first cars to arrive, but he hardly noticed. Instead of immediately jumping out, grabbing his kit bag from the boot, and jogging to the Owners, Trainers, and Jockeys Entrance as he usually did, Danny remained in his driver's seat, momentarily unable to summon the courage to leave the car.

There was good reason for Danny to delay. Today would be unlike any other race-day. Today, he was going to cheat.

Adjusting his rear-view mirror, Danny inspected himself. From the letterbox sized reflection a slightly receding blonde teenager, his hair shaved short, with a pinched, hollow face stared sullenly back at him. Two years of race-riding on the flat had certainly squeezed the youthfulness from his skin. Artificially maintaining the perfect racing weight of eight stone two pounds had seen to that. Gone was the rosy-cheeked sixteen-year-old who had topped the pony racing circuit. Despite being only a couple of months away from his twentieth birthday, Danny was inspecting a teenager old before his time. He rubbed his wizened chin thoughtfully, wondering whether his skin would ever lose its current clay-like pallor.

An involuntary shiver engulfed him, each ripple filling him with inglorious deceit. Danny shook himself, returning the mirror to its original position. It had to be done. He knew this to be true. Things had to change, and his ride today would mean he could start afresh.

At the entrance to Catterick racecourse, he waited nervously, but patiently, as an owner engaged in conversation with the ownership desk staff. Upon reaching the front of the queue he was rewarded with a broad smile from Sandra, the head gate-keeper to the restricted areas of the racecourse.

'Hello, Danny! Didn't I read that you're on seventy-four winners, only one away from turning professional?' she ventured from behind her desk as she recorded the extra owners badge he'd requested.

Danny returned her smile, a shade embarrassed. The bespeckled Sandra was in her early sixties, officious but always efficient, and tended to treat all the young jockeys with the same motherly attention.

'Thanks, Sandra, that's right.'

'You started your career here, didn't you, love?' she asked, after confirming the owners badge was booked and would be waiting for his guest.

Danny nodded, impressed with Sandra's knowledge of his riding history, 'I rode a horse called Last Rhapsody to win the final race on a Friday evening two years ago. It was my first ever winner.'

'I remember! The look on your face as you left that evening!' she reflected, cocking her head to one side thoughtfully.

'Well, the best of luck today, my darling,' she cooed, turning her attention to another customer who had just walked through the large glass doors.

Once into the racecourse proper, Danny found the Tattersalls area only sparsely populated with race-goers. It was to be expected, he'd arrived over an hour and a half before the first race – his race. Danny passed the empty parade ring and headed straight for the weighing room under the main stand, having no wish to encounter his boss, trainer Leo Fielding, or Francis Hibbert, the owner of the horse he was here to ride.

Leo had turned out to be a decent, but far from perfect choice in terms of his apprenticeship. The last twenty months had been frustrating and rewarding in equal measure. He'd been worked hard by Leo, but the trainer had supplied him with a steady source of rides, and a number of winners, albeit in low class events. Danny had ridden just over forty winners for Leo's Thirsk-based yard and on the whole, trainer and jockey had got along tolerably well. Leo wasn't fond of his apprentice's 'wasting' their preferential weight allowances by winning races on outside rides for other trainers. It was a stormy relationship, but outside rides apart, Leo was a fair boss and Danny rubbed along well enough with him. This was in stark contrast to the relationship Danny had with Francis Hibbert, the yard's biggest owner.

Hibbert, or 'Sir', as the retired millionaire insisted on being addressed, was a nightmare to deal with. He operated his string of fifteen racehorses with a strong hand and a distastefully ruthless disregard for the animals themselves. Once a horse lost favour with Hibbert, to his mind, it would no longer exist. He expected it to disappear immediately, both from the yard and from his training bills, with no regard for where it might end up. That was the trainer's problem, not his.

To Hibbert, horses were just a necessary evil in the pursuit of his primary objective; to give the bookmakers a good hiding. He was a prodigious gambler across many sports and despite his self-congratulatory stories of big wins, Danny was led to believe Hibbert's betting successes were heavily outnumbered by his losses.

As he owned a fifth of the total number of horses in Leo's yard, the trainer treated Hibbert with kid gloves, putting up with the man's constant demands for him to set up his horses for minor coups. Danny always listened with great interest as Leo dealt with Hibbert's tantrums around the stables or on the phone. When his owner was busy hectoring him, demanding to know when his next winning touch was going to land, the trainer used a combination of wily approaches.

Hibbert liked the sound of his own voice, and so allowing the millionaire to babble on with regular nods, affirming grunts, and a smile plastered to his face, whilst simultaneously telling 'Sir' that his request was impracticable, or simply impossible, worked some of the time.

On the odd occasion, Leo would have to agree to Hibbert's demands and aim a horse at a specific ill-judged race in the calendar that his owner had fixated upon. However, he would diligently plan the run, only for the animal to suddenly, and on some occasions, miraculously, develop some minor malady, such as a muscle pull, or not eating up a day or two before the intended race, and have to regretfully declare the poorly horse a non-runner.

'I can only get them race-fit and ready to win, I can't stop them getting a runny nose or straining a muscle,' Danny had heard Leo tell Hibbert on more than one occasion.

Finally, if everything else had failed, Leo would unleash upon 'Sir' the ultimate weapon in his training arsenal; unabashed, toe-curling flattery. Leo was a master at massaging and inflating Hibbert's ego. Some of his statements had Danny reeling at their preposterousness, yet Hibbert would suck the compliments into himself, as if through osmosis, and bask in his own wonderfulness.

The winners did come for Hibbert, but not always according to his own warped requirements. And when they won, trainer and jockey enjoyed an incredibly short-lived honeymoon period before 'Sir' decided he needed his next success. In private, Leo had likened Hibbert's gambling to a drug addict needing his next hit. When he had a big win and received ego-boosting compliments, it was like a double-whammy; Hibbert's version of ecstasy.

Hibbert would have been manageable if it wasn't for his biggest misconception. He believed that in order to achieve a big, bookie-bashing price on his horses, they should run a string of poor races before a win. It wasn't enough for him to simply win the race a horse had been set up for, they had to succeed at double-figure odds. It was an obsession. And he saw it as the jockey's job to ensure these 'poor runs' occurred prior to the winning run in order to fool the bookmakers into giving him his double-figure odds.

Hibbert had ear-marked today as a poor run.

On a regular basis Leo would attempt to explain to his owner that there were other ways of achieving this goal, and that these days bookmakers were more sophisticated in how they priced up a race, but this fell on Hibbert's deaf, self-righteous ears.

A combination of the wrong distance, unsuitable going, or an unsuitable track could have been sought out to achieve this outcome, and a fall in the horse's handicap mark, but there were occasions when Hibbert's belligerence won the day and on his insistence, the horse would run in a specific race unsuited to the result he required. These were the rides Danny hated with a vengeance, and he'd complained bitterly to trainer and owner alike on several occasions. He'd done the same only a few days ago when learning of today's run, and been provided with the same response; just do as you're told. Hibbert was determined. Danny had to ensure the horse he was riding today finished down the field.

Danny gloomily entered the weighing room and prepared himself. The race was the first on the card, a seven furlong claimer for juveniles, due off at 2-00pm. It was one of two rides he had on the day. He was set to ride Smashing Girl for Hibbert, a very nice two-year-old who had yet to show the talent she'd displayed at home in her two racecourse runs to date.

Hibbert had been adamant Smashing Girl would run at Catterick in this race. He had some people he wanted to entertain and having a runner would allow him to play at being their self-important host. Danny had broken into a cold sweat as soon as it was confirmed by the boss that he had booked him to ride. He was sure this was the right distance for the filly and the track that would suit her. She'd been crying out for this upping in trip and he would have his work cut out to make her look ordinary. It wasn't good enough to miss the kick and trail in last, the filly had to be seen to run a true race and appear to any onlooker, including the racing authorities, that the filly was at best, very moderate. Hibbert expected to see Smashing Girl jump cleanly, and with an energetic ride, finish tenth or eleventh in the twelve runner field, well beaten. This would ensure his filly received a lowly handicap mark when the official handicapper assessed her. Hibbert would then lump his money on her when making her handicap debut a few weeks later and purr like a cat when she won doing cartwheels.

It didn't help that for today's race Hibbert had chosen a lowly selling claiming race for her third run as a two-year-old. This heaped the pressure on Danny to conjure a poor performance from the filly against very moderate opposition.

It was a race where the weight your horse carried was dependent on a value in pounds sterling the owner had chosen as a claiming price for the filly. A sizeable claiming price would place a big weight burden on the horse, and vice-versa. Running in a selling claimer was always a gamble. Not only would the winning horse be sold, but any of the horses finishing in behind could be 'claimed'.

Anyone registered with the racing authorities could 'place a claim' after the race by agreeing to pay the advertised price for the horse, no matter where they finished. That was apart from the winner, who was instead subject to a public auction in the winner's enclosure after the race.

In a claimer, if there was more than one claim received for a horse, one of the claims was drawn at random and the lucky person got to buy the horse at the advertised price. You could run the risk of losing your horse if you placed too low a price on her, and she ran well. To add insult to injury, Hibbert had placed Smashing Girl in the race at the lowest possible claiming price, in order to make it appear she was indeed a racehorse of little note.

It was infuriating. Danny would basically be cheating on Hibbert's behalf. But he had no option… he was an apprentice, he had to follow instructions and finish his apprenticeship. Only then could he turn professional and be free of Leo and owners like Hibbert.

At 1-40pm Danny accompanied eleven other jockeys out of the weighing room, down the short walkway and into the parade ring, where Hibbert and Leo were standing waiting for him. Hibbert was a short, wide man who usually had a cigar rolling around his mouth. His dominant facial feature was a snub nose that flared when he was angry, thus displaying the internal contents of his hairy nostrils.

Leo, tall and lean, looked glum, whilst Hibbert greeted him with an outstretched hand and a broad grin. Behind the owner, a group of three shabbily dressed men looked on, seeming suitably impressed by their benefactor but somewhat uncertain of their surroundings. Two were heavy, middle-aged types, the third was much younger, gaunt, and boasted a bent nose and sharp eyes that were too close together to be anything other than weird.

'Danny!' Hibbert squeaked gleefully.

'Sir', he replied, touching the brim of his cap.

Indicating to his entourage they should come closer, Hibbert manufactured a small huddle around Danny.

'So you know the score here, lad,' Hibbert breathed.

'Yes, sir,' Danny confirmed, having found short, concise answers were best when addressing Hibbert.

'No showing off her ability, do you hear me?'

'I'll try my best.'

'No, lad. You won't try your best, you'll ride her like she's a donkey!' Hibbert said with a nasal laugh that came out as a snort. He'd turned to encourage his guests to join him in celebrating his clever control of horse and rider, but they either didn't agree, or more likely, were at a loss to understand. Danny got the impression the three men were a little out of their depth.

'I'm sure the filly will run an interesting race,' Danny said politely.

'I'm treating my staff today,' Hibbert explained, as an

uneasy silence followed Danny's words, 'They place bets for me all over the country when a horse of mine is set to win.'

'But not today!' he added with an exaggerated grin that raised nothing more than thin smiles from his guests.

That made sense, thought Danny as he cast a glance around at the three men. Two of them looked desperately uncomfortable and the other was staring wide-eyed at the massing crowd of faces watching them from behind the parade ring rails. He could imagine the three men lounging around in betting shops. This experience was well out of their comfort zone. All of them stood mute, hands dug into their jacket or jeans pockets.

Thankfully, the jockeys mount announcement was made and Danny and Leo were able to leave Hibbert and his trio of nervous men and move to the edge of the ring to wait for Smashing Girl to be led to them. Across the other side of the paddock the filly looked very well, was clearly fit, and jig-jogging on her toes, keen to get onto the racetrack.

'Thanks for that,' Leo said in a low voice as they waited, 'I had ten minutes of pure hell with them before you came out.'

'That's okay, boss.'

Two horses walked past them before Danny spoke again.

'Boss?'

'Yeah?'

'Are you sure you're okay with…'

'Of course,' Leo cut in, clapping his jockey lightly on his shoulder, 'Now come on, she's here. Just stick her on the heels of the two coming from stalls on the outside and she'll have nowhere to go. That's your ride.'

Danny was given a leg up and Leo backed away from the filly, his hands on his hips, watching his two-year-old head out onto the racecourse down the small chute in the corner of the parade ring. Danny took a long look over his shoulder at his boss before he started to hack down to the seven furlong start. He'd seen that look in his boss's eye once before. It was the same look Danny's father had given him on the platform of Bristol train station just before he'd set off to live and work in Thirsk when he was seventeen.

The filly felt powerful in his hands. She'd been a late developer, and immature in her opening two runs. Danny had no doubt she was a decent sort and Leo agreed, having always seen her as an autumn two-year-old who would blossom at three. She stretched out nicely as they cantered around the top of the course to the starting stalls and the fluidity of her movement brought a smile to Danny's lips. Hibbert was indeed about to witness an interesting race, just as he had promised.

Smashing Girl jumped well from her stall seven draw of the twelve runners, displaying a maturity that had been lacking in her runs to date. Instead of searching out the two poorest runners in the race, Danny tucked her into a share of fifth, one off the rails as they travelled along the top of the hill, and eased her into third before they reached the sharp top bend that would bring them into the straight and the three furlong run in to the finish.

Being a claiming race, there were a real mixture of abilities in the field, but one horse stood out on paper. Genial Graham had been an expensive purchase from the Book One Tatteralls yearling sales and had clearly been sent up from his leading Newmarket yard in order to get a win under his belt in lesser company than in the Class 4 maidens he'd previously been contesting. He was long odds on, and if that betting was correct, he was expected to win, not only easily, but by a country mile.

Danny held onto Smashing Girl, keeping the filly balanced around the bend, taking a tight route, ensuring there would still be finishing speed in reserve when they straightened up. At the point where he was supposed to be in behind horses, seemingly riding the filly along and going nowhere, Danny gave the filly a deft flick of his whip behind the saddle. For a split second he wondered what Hibbert might be thinking as Smashing Girl leapt forward, sauntering past a handful of horses in order to sit on the outside flank of the odds-on favourite.

Over two furlongs out, Danny got to work, crouching lower and pushing the filly forward. She was still green, and eyeballed Genial Graham on her inside as she drew alongside him at the furlong pole. Hitting the track undulations, Smashing Girl's challenge faltered slightly, but she fought on stoutly. The two youngsters remained locked together until the last stride, where the colt finally managed to assert himself by nosing ahead.

A look over Danny's shoulder showed Smashing Girl and Genial Graham had pulled eight to ten lengths clear of the third placed horse, and there was another five back to the rest of the field. When they pulled up, he gave the filly a congratulatory slap down her shoulder and cantered her back to the parade ring chute.

The filly's stable lass met them displaying a scared expression.

'You'd better run for the weighing room once you get off her, Danny,' she warned, 'Hibbert is spitting feathers about your ride. I left him screaming at Leo that you've made him look like a fool.'

Danny didn't have to wait until he slid off the filly's back to get a taste of Hibbert's wrath. The filly's owner was waiting for them as they reached the parade ring walkway and started to shout expletive ridden complaints up at his jockey as he followed them into the second placed slot in the winners enclosure.

Red in the face, spittle flying from his lips, Hibbert laid into Danny with loud, undisguised anger, prompting the large group of onlookers around the winners enclosure to stare at the small, rotund man with a mixture of shock and distaste. Danny ignored his owner, helping to undo the tack and slide his saddle off Smashing Girl. However, he didn't head immediately for the weighing room. Danny stood, saddle over his arm, and faced Hibbert and remained completely silent.

Such was his rage, in those first few minutes it was difficult to make out exactly the reason Hibbert was berating Danny. Many of the people who witnessed his tirade were under the impression he was apoplectic about not winning, but it soon became apparent this was not the case.

'What happened?' Hibbert spat, 'Forget who's the boss? Just remember who pay's your stinking wages and your riding fees you little…'

And so it went on, all manner of accusations and slurs interspersed with ripe language. Eventually, the filly was led away, and still Hibbert wasn't finished. Danny stared at the angry little man, tight-lipped and stony-faced.

After five minutes, Hibbert began to lose his thread, repeating himself and having to take long, gasping breaths between hurling abuse at his jockey. Throughout his owner's remonstrations, Danny remained completely mute. Hibbert was finally silenced by an announcement.

'As this race is a Selling Claimer, I will be conducting an auction of the winner, Genial Graham,' said a voice over the public address system.

Hibbert swung around and realised the winner was still in the enclosure and a chap on the winner's gantry was trying to elicit bids from the small crowd outside the rails.

'He eyed Danny and told him, 'Don't you move. I've not finished with you yet.'

Danny didn't acknowledge his demand; however, he remained rooted to the spot.

The bidding quickly reached ten thousand pounds before the hammer fell and the auctioneer declared the colt had been 'bought in' by its owner.

As a short presentation ceremony began for the winning connections, Hibbert was forced to drop his voice, but his intimidatory tone remained.

'You wanted to get your last winner, didn't you?'

Hibbert sneered, 'You wanted to be dead clever and reach seventy-five winners and screw me over while you did it!'

Danny breathed in, held it for a moment, and as he breathed out, he turned his head to the left and checked the time on one of the Tote screens. It was fourteen minutes past two.

'Well?' Hibbert demanded, his eyes wide.

Speaking in a soft, stern voice, Danny started to speak, never taking his eyes away from Hibbert's flushed face.

'Riding your racehorses over the last two years has been... a real education, sir. I wish to thank you from the bottom of my heart. I've been lucky enough to ride fourteen winners for you, and being in your company and listening to your sage advice and wise counsel has been extremely important, guiding me on my difficult journey through apprenticeship and into the professional realm.'

Hibbert's eyebrows dived into a flurry of furrows. Bewildered with Danny's response, he opened his mouth to reply, but found he was unable to find any suitable words. It was as if Danny's words had paralysed him. Until his brain could come to terms with what the jockey was saying, he was rendered speechless. Danny continued, singing the owner's praises in a manner that saw Hibbert dazzled by the eloquence of his flattery. And he said such wonderful things!

Exactly six minutes after he'd started, Danny brought his speech to its remarkable conclusion.

'Furthermore, I would like to thank you from the bottom of my heart for the time you have dedicated to nurturing my fledgling career. I've been humbled by your reaction to my ride today, and upon considering your timely advice, I will be retiring from the sport forthwith.'

Hibbert found himself half waving to his jockey like a King dismissing a courtier. Danny, straight-faced, gripped the brim of his helmet and tipped it deferentially to Hibbert. Behind the owner, Leo tried to control himself. He'd listened to the entire pantomime and was having to fight the urge to laugh out loud. He was astonished Hibbert had been taken in by Danny's brazen flattery, but then the boy's deadpan delivery had been masterful, and all the more impressive for one so young.

Danny turned his back on Hibbert and began to walk towards the exit of the parade ring, on his way to weigh back in. He was praying his nervousness didn't show, but he was convinced his timing had been just right…

The public address system crackled into life. A male voice made a racecourse-wide announcement to all race-goers, 'Following the two-o'clock seven furlong Selling Claimer, one claim was successful, second placed Smashing Girl was claimed by Mr D Vickers for eight-thousand pounds.'

Danny's heart leapt in his chest. Not daring to chance a look over his shoulder, he put his head down, held on tight to his saddle and tack, and broke into a swift walk. He sidled through the parade ring exit, and headed to the safety of the weighing room fifty yards in front of him down the tarmac walkway. He'd made it another twenty yards before the sound of running feet could be heard behind him. Ten yards before he reached his goal, the youngest of the three men accompanying Hibbert grabbed his shoulders from behind and brought him to a shuddering stop.

Danny was forcefully twisted around and met with a disgruntled scowl from the bent-nosed chap from Hibbert's entourage. His captor didn't say anything, but he held him tight, so tight Danny could feel the man's fingernails biting into his skin. Hibbert rolled up a few seconds later with the two older men and Leo, who loitered within listening distance wearing an amused grin.

'You claimed Smashing Girl?' Hibbert said incredulously, his eyes boring into Danny's.

For a moment he considered denying it, as in truth, he himself hadn't actually claimed the filly. However, a presence over Danny's left shoulder gave him the confidence to face his accuser and speak plainly.

'Yes, I claimed your racehorse,' Danny confirmed, shrugging off the hands still holding his shoulders. The young man tried instead to grip Danny's arm, but found his own wrist being grasped, restrained, and then twisted. Hibbert's man yelped when the sudden pain shot up his arm.

'Hands off my boy,' said a gruff voice, before shoving the squealing young man towards Hibbert.

'Who the hell…'

'This is my dad,' Danny cut in, 'David Vickers. He claimed Smashing Girl.'

A bemused Hibbert looked between Danny and then up at the powerful, six foot four man mountain that loomed over his son's shoulder.

'I take after my mother,' Danny added with an amused smile, hitching his saddle and tack up under his arm.

Before Hibbert could shape another round of accusations and expletive ridden demands, Danny confronted him face to face, standing as tall as he could, he defiantly locked eyes with the owner. He suddenly decided to drop his saddle in front of Hibbert, almost on the man's feet. It signalled his intentions perfectly. Hibbert glared down at the tack in shock.

'I've watched you ruin a dozen horses over the last two years in your attempts to land betting touches,' Danny said with undisguised distaste, pointing an accusatory finger at Hibbert, 'Running them too often to get their handicap marks down, making them race on bad, or bottomless ground, confusing them by teaching them to run down the field, then expecting they can go and win when you've got your money down… I became determined Smashing Girl would not go the same way. She's too talented. She could easily be ready for the scrap heap after you've messed around with her – like so many of the young horses unlucky enough to be bought by you.'

His confidence growing, Danny took a breath and continued, 'So I decided to save her. I rode her into second place today, knowing you'd blow a gasket when I got back into the parade ring. I let you talk…and talk. And then, I used flattery. I've been working on that despicable speech for weeks, timing it so that I could make sure that between your hissy fit over my ride, and listening to the ego fluffing rubbish I fed to you, the fifteen minute claiming window would close and you'd not be able to put in a friendly claim to get your horse back. My father and I now own the best horse that's ever gone through your hands, and because of the stupid games you play, you never even recognised you had a quality horse. I could have told you, your trainer tried to tell you, but you don't listen, do you? You always know best.'

Hibbert's flabby cheeks were burning red and his piggy eyes narrowed, lending his face a doughy, droopy quality. He regarded Danny with unconcealed contempt.

'I'll see to it you never ride for your boss again, or any trainer I have horses with,' Hibbert spat.

Danny returned a generous smile, 'I'll hit seventy-five winners. I've picked up a spare ride this afternoon, and what's more, I'll be winning on him. I don't need your horses, or Leo's yard! I'm my own man, and I've got jockey agents falling over themselves to represent me.'

'I'll report you!' Hibbert countered, a hint of desperation entering his tone.

'Go ahead,' Danny told him with a grin, 'There's no rules against my father claiming a horse. In fact, perhaps I'll tell the authorities about the instructions you gave me before the race and we'll see what they make of them?'

Hibbert paused, his attack momentarily blunted. He glanced around him. His three colleagues had quietly moved behind him during the latest argument, and they were now standing, heads down, inspecting their feet and shuffling further into the background. It was Leo who now stepped up and whispered in his owner's ear, only to be roughly pushed away. Leo shook his head, nodded toward Danny, and walked off. Danny started to do the same.

'Don't you dare move, Vickers!' Hibbert ordered.

Following a loud, minute-long volley of spiteful vitriol sprinkled with language that made racegoers from the surrounding area stare disbelievingly his way, Hibbert ran out of words once more and ground to a halt, gasping for air.

Danny grinned, then picked his saddle up from the tarmac, 'I'm about to walk into the weighing room, and you know what... *Sir*?'

Hibbert glowered, but didn't respond.

'When the Clerk of the Scales asks me why I'm so late and he disqualifies me for failing to weigh-in within the time allowed, I'll instruct him that my owner insisted I didn't weigh-in. That means you'll lose your prizemoney, and will face a fine by the authorities. And before you think you can squirm out of it, I have about fifteen witnesses,' Danny said, gesturing to the small crowd that had been watching Hibbert's performance.

With one final scowl, and a parting swearword that made some of the lady race-goers present audibly gasp, Hibbert turned on his heel and strode off.

A large hand landed on Danny's shoulder.

'Well done, lad,' said his father, 'When you told me about him, I thought you were gilding the lily. But he was even more detestable than I imagined. You've done well to put up with him for two years.'

'I was an apprentice jockey. That's what you have to do, Dad.'

An hour later Danny Vickers rode an odds-on favourite for a southern-based yard and in recording his seventy-fifth winner, lost his apprentice claim.

He then provided the on-course television crew and anchorman with an interview announcing that at the age of nineteen, not only was he no longer an apprentice, he was retiring from race riding.

'I've been battling with my weight for the last eighteen months and that's no way to live,' he told the shocked interviewer, 'I've got a Head Lad job offer in a good Lambourn yard that's going places and I start next week. The eventual goal is to be a trainer in my own right.'

Accompanied by his father, Danny set off to leave the racecourse after the fifth race. Sandra wished them well as they left, telling Danny, 'We'll miss you!'

'Tell me, son,' his father asked as they headed back to the car park, 'There's two things I'm a bit hazy about.'

Danny twisted his tight cheeks into a smile, 'Go on then, Dad.'

I know you stopped Hibbert from claiming his filly back by wasting his time, but couldn't anyone else have seen the run and claimed the horse?'

'They did,' Danny confirmed, 'But I had it covered. You were only one of four other people who put in a claim for Smashing Girl. Several trainers I've ridden for in the past put in claims on the filly on my behalf, just to be sure I got her. It just happened it was your name that came out of the bag at Weatherby's.'

His father raised an eyebrow.

'And something else…' he murmured, 'What would have happened if you'd won on the filly?'

'She'd have been bought back by Hibbert,' Danny replied immediately, keeping his eyes focused on the path ahead.

Father and son walked on in silence for a few steps.

'So, did you…?'

'Smashing Girl will get the chance to have a proper racing career,' Danny replied, shooting his father an earnest stare, 'And I suppose we were just lucky that she finished second, otherwise the odious Mr Hibbert would have got the chance to buy her back at the auction.'

The older man shook his head and smiled ruefully, 'You're just like your mother,' he said with an arched eyebrow, 'You've always got a plan.'

Danny reached his car, dropped his kit bag into the

trunk and turning to face his father, stepped forward and gave him a hug. When he released him, his eyes were sparkling.

'It's just as well I'm like her, Dad,' he said happily, 'If I was like you, six foot four and weighing over eighteen stones, I doubt I'd have been in demand as an apprentice jockey.'

Freddie's Free Four-Timer

One

March 5th 2021

Considering it was a cold, wet Friday evening, Freddie's mum was pleased her son was unexpectedly perky at teatime. Mrs Wilson gave an infinitesimal shake of her head, silently scolding herself. The weather was the least of Freddie's worries. Covid restrictions had tipped his life upside down, and despite Boris Johnson promising the rules on meeting friends would be eased in ten days' time, the last few months had hit her son's confidence pretty hard. It wasn't just Freddie, after all, along with his younger half-sister Amelia, the three of them had been holed up in their two-bedroomed terrace for almost four months now. Mrs Wilson couldn't remember the last time both her children had been able to meet and play with their friends.

Mrs Wilson watched Freddie wolf his tea down, the small folding tin table they used for all their meals rattling as he dug in. Whatever the reason, it was good to see her normally quiet seventeen-year-old demolish his fish-fingers, oven chips, and peas as if he'd never been fed. He excused himself, and without waiting for a reply, raced up the stairs, taking three of the tight, thin steps at a time, and slammed his bedroom door shut. Amelia and Mrs Wilson waited, their eyes trained on the ceiling. They heard a squeak, and a soft thump from the floorboards above as Freddie landed in his chair in front of the old laptop they all shared, and then scraped himself forward until he banged into the makeshift computer desk made from a trio of discarded pallets Freddie had cleverly fixed together.

Nine-year-old Amelia broke the silence, 'He's on a Zoom call with all his mates again,' she said with a disappointed sigh. She placed a forkful of fish-finger in her mouth and chewed in a disgruntled manner, 'It's their Talent Night… er, Club.'

Mrs Wilson rolled her eyes at the youngster, 'Don't talk with your mouth full. And what do you know about zooming around night clubs?'

Amelia swallowed and looked sullen for a moment, but then frowned at her mother.

'Aw, come on, Mum!' she cried, not sure whether her mum was kidding her or not, 'You know what I mean…'

'Yes, I was fooling with you,' Mrs Wilson said with a crafty smile, 'Just remember that Freddie is almost eighteen, and it's been tough on your brother, not being able to go to school, or see his friends, just like it has for you.'

'It means I can't go on the internet for two hours,' Amelia complained, her sullen look returning.

'You'll get your turn on the laptop,' Mrs Wilson promised, patting her daughter's hand and rising to clear the dinner plates from the rickety kitchen table.

Upstairs, Freddie watched with a tingle of anticipation as one by one, his schoolmates joined the weekly video conferencing session. There could be anything up to thirty-five of his Year Thirteen schoolmates logging on for the Friday virtual Talent Night. It was his last year at College, with A-Level exams looming, although the chance of him sitting any meaningful exams looked remote, thanks to the pandemic and the loss of face to face teaching. His future was hanging in the balance and there was little he could do to materially affect it in any significant way. Everything he'd worked for was now dependent on which direction the politicians and faceless examination executives decided to go. So, the chance to spend a couple of hours forgetting it all was incredibly inviting.

Slowly, his laptop screen filled with teenagers. He knew all their names, but there were a number of them he'd never had the chance to meet properly, which he always found quite daunting. However, he was waiting for one specific user to pop up; Elizabeth Wilhelmina Green.

'It's Minnie,' the girl with a round face, short black hair and deep, hazel eyes you could become lost in, had informed him the only time they'd ever met. She'd raised an amused dark eyebrow and her lips had curled up on one side in such a way, Freddie had lost the power of speech for several seconds.

Minnie insisted on being addressed with this corrupted version of her middle name. And that wasn't the only difference that marked her out as a rebellious teen. Whereas most girls in his year group had long hair, heavily made-up faces, and filled their social media channels with selfies of themselves pouting, or in poses that made Freddie desperate to post sarcastic comments, Minnie sported the lightest touches of make-up, and wore rock band tour t-shirts, leather skirts, fishnet stockings, and doc martins. She posted reviews of books she'd read, and photos of the promotional posters for the weird independent films she was currently watching, although she also admitted to being a sucker for tongue-in-cheek romcoms too. She commented on politics, food with meat (no vegan stuff for her!), and she admitted to having a soft-spot for nineteen-fifties and sixties science fiction; the true genesis of modern sci-fi, as she described it on her Facebook page.

Freddie was smitten. He had been from the moment he'd tripped over her Dockers, crashed into her lap, and looked up into those soulful eyes. Telling himself it was just an infantile crush, he had tried to rid his mind of her perfect physical features and intelligent, confident speech. It had proved an impossible task.

Everything about the girl was just right – even though they'd only met once in person. His chance to meet her again had been cruelly stolen by the Covid crisis. The school year had been a mess. It had begun with lost classes, then the entire year group had been sent home. They'd returned for a matter of days, only to be sent home once more. As the full lockdown was announced, Freddie had finally been dispatched home again to spend the long winter months being virtually schooled.

Minnie was in the other half of the year group and he'd bumped into her, quite literally, in an A-Level English Language lesson, their only class together. He'd tripped over her feet attempting move along a row in the lecture theatre. And after an initial 'Ouch!' and apologies, she'd smiled, and they'd talked. A short, five sentences that he had now committed to memory and replayed every night before he fell asleep. If anything, Covid had exacerbated his lack of confidence and longing to spend time with Minnie, as she was now unattainable, being nothing more than a head and shoulders in a small box on his laptop once a week.

The computer played a loud bong and the words, JIMMY: 'Freddie Boy!' screamed at him in angry text from the private messaging section of his Zoom meeting screen. One of the features of the Zoom software was to allow members of a meeting to message each other with text whilst other people were talking.

Jumping forward in his hard kitchen chair, Freddie focused on the small square window that would be flashing at him. He clicked on the tiny image of a grinning head on a blue background and his best friend expanded to fill a quarter of the laptop's screen. Jimmy's hang-dog face, tousled hair, and fiercely bright blue eyes immediately made Freddie smile.

Taking a moment to make sure it was just the two of them having a one-to-one text conversation, Freddie grinned back at his mate.

FREDDIE: 'Jimmy! And how are you this fine Covid evening?' he typed.

JIMMY: 'I'm right up for it tonight, Fred,' Jimmy returned. Freddie looked at the silent video feed of his friend beaming, bobbing around on his seat whilst running a hand through his unruly hair. He looked down, typing again.

JIMMY: 'Steve Frost ain't gonna beat me this week.'

Freddie gave a little laugh and shook his head. Steve

Frost ran the talent night, was terribly popular, and undeniably talented. It seemed there wasn't a sport, subject, instrument, or pastime in which he couldn't claim to be proficient.

FREDDIE: 'You been working on your act?'

JIMMY: 'Oh yes! Damn right I have! And don't call it an act! It's not an act, it's an *experience*!'

He looked up and into his webcam once he'd finished typing, and added an exaggerated roll of his eyes.

FREDDIE: 'You know it's not supposed to be that serious.'

Jimmy appeared to groan from his mute little box on Freddie's screen.

JIMMY: 'Tell that to Frosty.'

Every person on the Talent Night zoom call could take their turn to take the stage – usually in their bedroom – and perform anything they wanted to the virtual audience. The idea was that each week up to a dozen people would take the opportunity to entertain the rest of Year Thirteen for a couple of minutes. It was all done for fun, and no-one had been booed off… yet. Each performance would prompt all manner of laughter, questions, reactions, sometimes derision, and always discussion. Finally, everyone would salute the performer, have a glug of a drink at their side, and the focus would move on to the next person's virtual talent presentation.

You could do anything you wanted. Often people would play a musical instrument, karaoke along to a song, maybe even dance, a couple of the lads had even tried to do a standup routine. Many people, especially the girls, would go for the obvious singing, but there were those with more fertile imaginations who would come up with some incredible ideas. Of course, the more outrageous, crazy, and silly their two to three minute performance was, the more everyone would enjoy themselves.

This was the fifth virtual talent night. So far, Freddie

had performed twice, mainly due to Jimmy insisting he did something and to stop being such a wuss. Thankfully, his first effort had gone down quite well. He'd kicked off with an easy one: singing over Neil Diamond's 'Sweet Caroline' and Jimmy had encouraged everyone to sing along and wave their arms about during the choruses.

His most recent two minute performance had made him so nervous, he'd thrown up before he performed. In the end, Jimmy had come around to the house, flouting the Covid regulations, in order to force him to get up and do it. He'd quietly explained he was a resident at a zombie retirement home. Wearing a zombie mask and playing 'The Timewarp' from The Rocky Horror Show in the background, Freddie had proceeded to start dancing... badly. He'd been careful to wear a pair of his mother's shocking pink marigold gloves and after dancing around a little had allowed one of the gloves, stuffed with newspaper, to drop off, eliciting a generous laugh from his virtual audience when he came to a sudden halt, looked quizzically at the stump, shrugged, and continued to dance. A few seconds later the other hand wobbled, fell off, and hit the floor. Finally, Freddie had dropped to his knees, yelling, 'Oh no, that's my feet gone!' and reached forwards out of camera shot to hold up two fake legs. He'd made them by filling a pair of his mother's old tights with newspaper and stuffing them into an old pair of trainers. They'd looked nicely realistic, especially being held in the bloody stumps of his hands (tomato soup dipped in tissues). He'd been particularly pleased that Minnie had been smiling and laughing appreciatively at the end of his performance. But that was enough, he couldn't face that sort of pressure anymore, so he'd not done a performance for a month.

FREDDIE: 'So come on, Jimmy, are you ready?'

Jimmy screwed his face up and nodded.

JIMMY: 'Think so. Really hoping Frosty the no-man is going to be green with envy.'

Freddie knew where Jimmy's competitive battle for

supremacy over fellow Year Thirteen student, Steve Frost, came from. The two of them had been competing against each other for the last two years. It was centred on their shared obsession for the voluptuous Olivia Freeman, the most dateable girl in the year. Annoyingly, every time the subject arose, Jimmy would look at Freddie quizzically and claim she had nothing to do with his private battle with Steve.

Freddie secretly thought Jimmy and Steve were quite similar, and this was the reason they butted heads so often, especially over Olivia Freeman. Both of them were happiest in the limelight, to the point of being exhibitionists. And yet any mention of this possibility had Jimmy denying it in the strongest terms. So, as a dutiful friend, Freddie steered clear of the subject as best he could.

However, Jimmy's similarity to Steve Frost did diverge radically in terms of his background. Steve lived in an expensive area of Leeds and at least on the surface, appeared to enjoy a life free of money worries. He wore the latest fashions, had an expensive haircut, was the first student to arrive at college in a car, and spoke with an accent that merely suggested he was a lad from Leeds.

Meanwhile, Jimmy and Freddie enjoyed less salubrious council-owned accommodation and spoke like proper Leeds United supporters. Living only a few doors apart on the back-to-back terrace that was Osborne Street, they had been friends for as long as they could remember. They both shared their bedroom with their siblings, and also shared a similar family set-up, complete with absent fathers. In Freddie's case, he'd never known his father. Jimmy's had left over a decade ago, although he still made awkward visits on his birthday.

Jimmy and Freddie also seemed to share the same problem at the moment; being incapable of capturing the attention of the girls they were currently obsessing over.

Presently, the small windows on Freddie's laptop became populated with many more tiny faces as they drew closer to the start time of talent night. Freddie's pulse quickened when a familiar orange background and a round, dark face offset with a perfect ring of bright white teeth entered the Zoom session.

He stared at the small square containing the girl with the smile and shiny olive skin and wondered whether tonight would present him with the opportunity to share that long overdue second conversation with her. This thought prompted a swirling in his stomach. A heady mixture of Freddie's crumbling confidence and painful longing combined to create a physical response. He clamped his arms tightly to his sides as perspiration began to flow freely from his armpits.

Two

Almost two hours later, Steve Frost brought the virtual talent night to a close with a short speech in his own, supremely confident style. One by one, the small faces in windows started to wink out of existence as members of the year group made their excuses and logged off. It had been an entertaining couple of hours, the highlights being Greg Mallory's rendition of 'My Way' and, to Freddie's delight, Jimmy's short story.

Greg had sung along to Disney's 'The Wonderful Thing About Tiggers' from the Winnie The Poo movie, whilst bouncing on a trampoline in his back garden. Thanks to a combination of weighing north of eighteen stones and being slightly tipsy, he'd managed to lose his balance, bounced torpedo-like head-first off the trampoline, and out of range of his laptop's camera. This had elicited a mixture of laughs and worried gasps from his audience. Groggily emerging back on camera moments later, mud stained and looking bewildered, Greg had received a round of applause.

He went on to tell everyone he'd landed in a flower bed, but was determined to finish his song. He'd belted out the last few lines and reached the 'I'm the only one...' bit when his eyes bulged and he held a hand to his mouth. Having dashed off-camera Greg's audience was treated to the sounds of him groaning and being sick. His finale consisted of him staggering back onto camera with a bottle of beer in his hand and screaming, 'Cheers!' before losing his balance once again and landing on his backside with a silly grin on his face. The laughing took a minute and a half to subside, and someone had been recording it, so it was played back a couple of times for everyone to enjoy again. Freddie wasn't too surprised when the video surfaced on YouTube later that evening.

Jimmy delivered his short story perfectly. His ability as an orator shone through, and his hours of practice paid off handsomely. He'd found his short story on the internet. Written by a student in her first year of university, it was a simple story, that spanned only one week during lockdown, detailing all the experiences, expectations and hopes lost to her generation as a result of the pandemic. Jimmy had held his audience right from the first line, all the way through to its conclusion. Freddie knew the story backwards, as Jimmy had been practicing on him every day for the last week, so during his friend's short recital he'd chosen to concentrate on the faces of the audience, rather than watching his best friend. He was pleased when some of the year group smiled, even more so when they became still and thoughtful. There were even a couple of tears wiped away from the eyes of one or two of the female listeners after Jimmy had delivered the last line. It had definitely touched a number of the students present.

Afterwards, there had been a short, but complete silence from the thirty-eight talent night attendees. Freddie had waited with breath bated as Jimmy looked nervously into his webcam, concern at the lack of an immediate response writ large in his friend's eyes. But when it came, the reaction proved to be a torrent of genuinely warm positivity, mixed with a dash of amazement that Jimmy had delivered the tale with such maturity. It was very different to his persona at college, where he was known for playing the fool. Freddie had watched with reflected pride as his friend was praised from all sides, and to Freddie's surprise, Jimmy blushed bright red as he received these plaudits.

Steve Frost wasn't among Jimmy's supporters, and he visibly scowled once Olivia declared how delightful the story was, and the sensitivity of Jimmy's performance. She'd delivered this review in a husky, and some might say, suggestive manner.

Once the talent night had moved on to a girl singing along to a Lily Allen hit, Jimmy had messaged Freddie.

JIMMY: 'I think we stuck it to Frosty tonight!'

FREDDIE: 'I think YOU stuck it to him… His juggling act was dire.'

JIMMY: 'Couldn't have done it without you. Cheers mate.'

FREDDIE: 'Have to say, Olivia was VERY impressed with you tonight.'

JIMMY: 'Oh right.'

FREDDIE: 'Frosty's face was a picture.'

JIMMY: 'Didn't really notice!'

However, he added several smiley faces.

Freddie read this last comment from his friend three times. He wrote two different replies, and deleted them, unhappy with them. In the end, he didn't reply at all. For whatever reason, Jimmy refused to be drawn on the subject of Olivia and Steve Frost, so there was little point in pursuing it with him.

One of the last people to perform was Rick Worlsey, a quietly spoken boy with a mop of blonde hair and a face unfortunately severely spotted with acne. His couple of minutes wasn't so much a performance, more an announcement. Given they were all stuck at home, looking for things to do, he ran through half a dozen suggestions to spend time that week getting free, interesting things over the internet. He talked about a small website where you could play this word game called 'Wordle', that he claimed was novel and addictive. He also recommended a couple of podcasts, one featuring Bob Mortimer that Freddie thought he'd try out. Rick also shared a link to a national bookmaker's website that allowed anyone over the age of eighteen to have a completely free bet – something called an accumulator. Rick explained you just had to choose four events in 2021 and try to pick the winners. Freddie bookmarked this link, not too sure what was meant by 'an accumulator', and immediately forgot about it when Steve Frost announced Minnie Green was the last act of the night.

Freddie watched in a bubble of adoration as Minnie introduced her two minute performance. She explained it was an animation she had been working on for the last three weeks, and hoped people liked it. A short story in the Manga style, it followed a young girl at school, crying when she was bullied by a bigger boy. After several attempts, she eventually stood up to her bully and was victorious in a fight. However, the short story ended with a twist, when the young girl realised her bully was now crying himself. The young girl had then thought hard, eventually going to him and consoling her one-time enemy.

The cartoon was a big hit, and the perfect way to round off the evening. Minnie received lots of praise, Freddie among them, all of which she accepted with a tight smile. He sat back, enjoying the sensation of his stomach flipping over every time he looked longingly at the enlarged oblong of video containing Minnie's head and shoulders.

Perhaps it was Jimmy's success that spurred him on, or the bravery of the character in Minnies animation, or possibly the three shots of vodka he'd drunk in the last half hour. Whatever the reason, Freddie steeled himself, and wrote a short private message to Minnie, saying he thought the animation was wonderful and would love to discuss it in more detail. He quickly tapped the send icon, not wishing to give himself time to think too deeply about the pros and cons of such an approach, and waited nervously for a reply.

He was left pensively watching the cursor blinking pointlessly in his send message box for the next twenty seconds. After thirty seconds Freddie checked Minnie was still on the video call - she was - there were only four people left in the Talent Night meeting, including Steve Frost, himself, and Minnie. Still no reply after a minute… then a set of three dots began to pulse, sending Freddie's heart thumping in his chest – she was composing a reply. Finally, after another ten second wait, Minnie's answer was displayed.

MINNIE: Thanks.

Freddie waited another thirty seconds in the hope there would be a follow-up message, but the three pulsing dots stubbornly refused to blink. That was it… one word that didn't come close to fulfilling his wretched need for communication with her. She might as well have slapped him in the face. It was a devastatingly clear sign she had absolutely zero interest in him. He logged off the Talent Night meeting in a daze of self-pity.

Three

May 7th 2021

Jimmy lay on Amelia's bed, his big, stocking feet poking over the end of the child's sized mattress and stared mournfully up at Freddie's bedroom ceiling. Freddie lay a few feet away on his own bed, doing the same. They were being bored together on a dreary Friday afternoon. Lockdown was still preventing them from meeting more than close friends in their 'bubble' and the latest news from college had plunged both of them into a state of depressed lethargy.

'I used to look forward to Friday nights,' Freddie moaned, 'At least we had the talent night.'

Jimmy pursed his lips together and mumbled his

agreement.

'Why did Steve stop doing them?' Freddie continued.

He was trying his best to get Jimmy to emerge from the funk he'd been in for the last two weeks – anything to get him talking.

'There's no exams and no college any more,' Jimmy offered.

'Yeah, but he could have continued them anyway.'

There was a short pause before Jimmy filled the silent void.

'He and Olivia are an item. According to her Instagram account they are both off to Leeds to do music together. At the moment, they're busy looking for flats.'

Freddie sat up on one elbow and peered over at Jimmy in the bed against the far wall, half a foot lower than him.

'Frosty's already got a place at University?'

'Yeah.'

'Who told you?'

'Facebook,' Freddie replied quietly. He didn't move his head, still inspecting the contours of the white stippled ceiling with its hundreds of hanging meringue-like swirls, 'They both got unconditional offers. It's plastered all over Olivia's page too.'

Once again, the conversation dried up for a short time.

'Is it just me that has a sense of unfinished business?' Freddie cried plaintively.

'How do you mean?'

Freddie got up and crossing over to the desk, pushed the power button on his laptop, 'You know, no exams, no final day at the college... and now, no prom... it's like we've been left in limbo.'

Jimmy gave an exaggerated sigh and covered his face with his hands.

'I can't believe they cancelled prom,' he complained from behind his hands.

Another heavy, thoughtful silence ensued, both of the

teenagers considering the implications of the loss of this final chance to meet with their year group face to face before everyone left for jobs, apprenticeships, or further education.

'It doesn't seem right,' moaned Freddie, 'Our teachers will send an assessment to some faceless adjudicator and in a month's time we'll get a flipping message – a soulless email! - that will tell us we're either a hero or a zero. And we don't get to see anyone from college, or even say goodbye. Too risky and too expensive, the college said… too much like they can't be bothered! Covid has cheated us out of a year, no… eighteen months of our lives. Maybe the most important time of our lives!'

'And now it's cheating us out of a prom…' Jimmy added in a soft, dejected voice.

The laptop sprang into life with a ping and Freddie went to the desk to investigate – anything to distract him from the sullen atmosphere in his bedroom. The noise also elicited movement from Jimmy. He intentionally rolled off Freddie's sister's bed, landing with a soft thump on the paper thin carpet covering the floorboards. He lay there, inert for a few seconds. Finally, a loud groan proceeded him getting to his feet, and dusting himself off. He pushed out his lips, and frowned.

'Go on… tell me that email is to say they've cancelled Christmas,' he said mournfully.

Freddie studied his friend as his laptop quietly clicked whilst loading his internet email account. He might not be depressed, but Jimmy was definitely… he searched for the right word… morose. That was it, even though they could get together now and go for walks in the park, Jimmy was morose, like all the fun had been squeezed out of him. He had an idea as to the cause, but he knew his friend too well… there would a right time to mention it.

'What's that about?' Jimmy said with a frown, touching his fingertip to a line of text on the screen, 'You haven't been gambling have you?'

Switching his gaze back to the screen, Freddie examined the title of the email. It read, 'Paid Promotional Opportunity' and was from someone with an email address that read Josh.Scott@falstaffbookmakers.com.

'It'll be spam,' he assured his friend.

Freddie opened the email and together, they read the contents.

Dear Mr Wilson,

As you will be aware, the second of your selections in your 'Free Falstaff Accumulator' was successful last weekend. Congratulations!

Although you still have two selections yet to be settled, I wish to offer you £1,200 to complete some promotional work for Falstaff Bookmakers. Please contact me on the telephone number below, or video call me for more information.

Yours sincerely,
Mr Josh Scott,
Marketing Manager.

'What the hell? It has to be spam,' Freddie concluded.

'Nope, I think it's real!'

There was a sort of excitement in Jimmy's voice that hadn't been there for the last couple of weeks. Freddie read the message again.

'Call the number!' exclaimed Jimmy excitedly.

'Hold on, let me check this out.'

Two minutes later Freddie was inspecting his online account with Falstaff Bookmakers, having dug out his welcome email from the company the month before.

'It's that link Rick sent us for the free bet.'

'I never got round to doing it,' Jimmy admitted.

'You had to choose a selection from four events and create an account. I think I had to pick some horses in important races, and something else…'

The laptop screen flickered and an account page opened

displaying one open bet. Freddie clicked on it and the two friends studied the contents of the screen:

Accumulator – Stake £3 – FREE BET

1. The Grand National, April 5th 2021
Selection: *Minella Times* - Odds: 33/1 – **WON**

2. 2000 Guineas, May 7th 2021
Selection: *Poetic Flare* - Odds: 25/1 – **WON**

3. The Derby, June 2nd 2021
 Selection: *Adayar* - Odds: 25/1 – NOT SETTLED

4. GB Snow on Christmas Day, 25th December 2021
Selection: *YES* - Odds 9/1 – NOT SETTLED

Jimmy whistled his appreciation, 'How on earth did you manage to find those two winners?'

Freddie didn't answer. Jimmy repeated his question.

'I… can't even remember,' Freddie said uncertainly, his brow knitted into a deep frown.

Jimmy did a quick sum in his head.

'Crikey Fred, you've already got over £1,500 running onto your selection in the Derby!'

He picked up a pencil from the makeshift desk and wrote a few calculations on a scrap of paper. He checked them through again. When he looked round at his best friend, he was wearing a wide-eyed, silly grin.

'If the other two selections win,' Jimmy said with his excitement growing, 'You'll collect… over five-hundred and fifty thousand pounds in winnings.'

Freddie shook his head, 'There's no way that will happen. I chose these horses and… the Christmas thing at random. It was after we'd had one of those talent nights and I'd had a few too many shots of vodka.'

Jimmy slapped his friend on the back, 'Doesn't matter

how you picked them, mate, you're half-way to big money.'

Twenty minutes later Freddie hung up his call to Josh Scott of Falstaff bookmakers. Jimmy had listened to the conversation on loudspeaker.

'You're going to do it?' Jimmy asked, barely able to contain himself.

Freddie pushed his lips together as he considered.

'Come on Fred,' Jimmy protested, 'It's a grand for a few photos!'

'Oh, I'm going to do it, ' Freddie grinned, 'What I'm wondering is whether one-thousand two-hundred quid would buy us a venue for a Year Thirteen College prom!'

Four

May 14th 2021

To Freddie's eye, the Falstaff Bookmakers shop on the high street looked decidedly tatty. Just like practically every other shop on the high street, it was closed. There was no way a bookmaker could qualify as 'an essential service' under the current Covid rules.

Standing in front of the huge window, he and Jimmy peered between tall, free-standing cardboard adverts detailing out-of-date football and horse racing events and into the shop beyond. It was dark, vacant, and uninviting.

'This is definitely the place?' Jimmy queried.

Freddie nodded, 'I checked it twice. This is the address.'

A small silver-haired woman struggling with a carrier bag full of milk and bread passed them. In her free hand a complaining six-year-old child was being dragged along by his parka hood. Momentarily flicking her eyes up at the two lanky teenagers with masks covering most of their faces, the woman scolded the youngster, put her head down, and hurried past the boys.

'I bet we look like a pair of bank robbers,' Freddie said, watching the women and child scurry away from them.

'What do you mean?'

'Standing here, with masks covering our faces, hanging around a shop that's closed and not likely to open any time soon!'

'Yeah, I guess. Never thought of it that way.'

'The sound of keys jangling and a steel latch being drawn back signalled the bookmaker's shop wasn't as empty as they'd imagined. The two friends swung round and were greeted by a corpulent middle-aged man with a jet-black comb-over.

'You the lad with the acca?'

'Erm... yeah,' Freddie replied.

The man pulled the steel-rimmed door open and stepped back, and rumbled, 'Best come in then.'

Locking the door behind them, the man slowly led them through the darkness of the shop, behind the service counter, and into a smaller, well-lit room at the back of the building. At one end cardboard boxes containing betting slips were poorly stacked against a wall, a few stray slips littering the concrete floor. At the other side of the room a number of professional-looking lights were pointed at a large canvas backdrop covered in Falstaff Bookmaker logos. Two men stopped what they were doing and looked up at Freddie and Jimmy. The first wore chinos and crocs, and had an expensive-looking camera strung around his neck. The second man was young, probably early twenties, and was wearing a tight-fitting blue suit. He leapt forward, a maniacal grin on his face, and stuck a hand out, before immediately retracting it.

'Sorree... Forgot! Social distancing and all that!'

Freddie looked at the set-up and quelled the urge to immediately run for the door.

'You got the money?' he asked.

'I'm Josh,' the suited man said, ignoring Freddie's question, 'And you must be Frederick?'

'Freddie,' Freddie corrected, 'Freddie Wilson', and this is my friend, Jimmy Jones.'

'Good to meet you both,' Josh said, plastering a plastic grin onto his face for good measure.

The fat chap who had let them into the shop was now leaning against the wall with his arms crossed. He remained there, radiating boredom.

Josh got Freddie to sign a marketing agreement and for the next ten minutes he was made to pose for a huge number of photos, Jimmy smirking as his friend was made to smile like a shark whilst holding an over-sized betting slip with his free four-timer selections printed on them. Jimmy eventually became bored and tried to engage the fat bloke in conversation, but soon regretted it. He uncovered the fact that he was talking to the manager of this betting shop, but the chap was clearly in no mood for small-talk.

Once the photographer signalled he had enough material, Josh got out a notepad. He explained he needed a few bits of personal information from Freddie in order to construct a story they could publish with the photos.

'There's enough bad news around with Covid, and with our betting shops shut, we're desperate for a bit of good news,' Josh was at pains to explain, 'A free bet possibly netting a customer hundreds of thousands of pounds will be a positive story and might drive a few more people to have a bet on our website.'

'Speaking of revenue,' Jimmy called from the back of the room, 'When does Freddie get his money?'

Josh waved Jimmy's enquiry away and asked a few more questions before dipping into his inside pocket and producing a wad of twenty pounds notes.

'Twelve-hundred pounds, in cash, as agreed,' he advised Freddie, 'What will you spend it on?'

Freddie took the cash, considered counting it, but thought better of it, 'It's going to pay for our year at college to get a prom.'

Freddie was surprised when Josh expressed delight upon learning this news. He couldn't help feeling a shade uneasy as the marketing man scribbled notes furiously on his notepad.

Five

May 19th 2021

The news of 'Freddie's Free Four-Timer' was published on the Falstaff Bookmakers website the following Monday, along with an embarrassingly toothy photo of him holding a giant betting slip. It also made it onto the Evening Press website. However, it wasn't until Jimmy and Freddie announced a day later that the money would be used to host their own Year Thirteen prom, that the news of the bet began to go viral around Leeds.

It started with Jimmy doing several social media posts, and a few friends shared it around that everyone from Year Thirteen was invited to a prom a few days after the date Prime Minister, Boris Johnson, was expected to announce would be the final stage four relaxation in Covid restrictions. It would allow them to hold a prom with more than the current limit of thirty people attending. This was shared around, then the news of the free bet got mixed in and shared to an even wider audience. The internet around Leeds was soon trending about the kids whose prom was cancelled and who were now going to stage their own prom for their entire year group. And it was all thanks to a free Covid lockdown bet!

Josh had apparently been right on the money. When good news is in short supply, even the remotest possibility of a teenager winning over half a million pounds from a free bet was of interest to the media. They pounced on the story.

At first it was exciting to be in demand. Soon, it was overwhelming. Freddie and Jimmy were receiving invites to be interviewed by journalists from all over the UK. It wasn't so much the bet, but the fact Freddie and Jimmy wanted to host their own prom, after being left without the opportunity to say goodbye face to face to the other sixty people in the year. It seemed there were a huge number of students up and down the country sharing the same frustrations, namely of being short-changed by Covid and their school or college.

They'd already done half a dozen phone and video interviews when Freddie got the fateful call from Look North. The regional BBC One news programme was watched by millions every evening. The producer got in touch and said he wanted to get them on Zoom and Linda Stubbins would interview them live that evening. Freddie and Jimmy had no option. They said yes.

The interview was going well, with Jimmy and Freddie bouncing nicely off each other in a jokey sort of way. Having been interviewed a dozen times over the last twenty-four hours, they'd almost got a little act going, as every interviewer had asked virtually the same questions. Then Linda, the anchor in the television studio, smiled at the teenagers and asked her next question.

'So, Freddie, what led you to choose your selections in your free four-timer bet?'

In the heat of the moment and without thinking, Freddie answered, 'They were inspired by a special person.'

As soon as he'd heard the words coming from his mouth he knew he'd made a big mistake. Jimmy gave him a surprised glance. Freddie's stock answer to that question thus far had been that his selections had been completely random, so this was news to him too. Linda smiled benignly, and with growing dread Freddie knew she would follow up with the only possible next question.

'So who's that special person, Freddie?'

Freddie squirmed in the seat they'd set up in his living room in front of the open fire, and sweat burst forth from his forehead and under his arms.

'Yes, Freddie,' echoed Jimmy with a devilishly cruel smile, obviously amused by this development, 'Tell the audience of millions out there who inspired your winning selections.'

Freddie shot him a dark look, whilst his mind searched desperately for an answer, any answer but the real one. He was suddenly aware of the clock on the wall ticking loudly in the silence. His eyes darted around and came to rest on his mother and sister who were standing behind the laptop camera with eyes wide, gesticulating, willing him to answer. Still he didn't reply and a few more seconds of pure hell ensued as Freddie, open mouthed, struggled desperately for inspiration. Linda began to look a little testy, getting ready to move the interview on, or cut it short. Meanwhile, Jimmy was beaming, finding the situation incredibly funny.

'Well, this person must be *very* special...' Linda said in a 'wrapping-up the interview' sort of way.

'My Mum!' Freddie barked, 'It was my... Mum.'

By now, Linda had picked up on Jimmy's mirth, and wasn't going to allow an opportunity like this to pass, despite her interviewee cringing with embarrassment.

'Really? She told you which horse would win the Grand National and the 2,000 Guineas? She must really love her horse racing.'

He didn't know where it came from, but from somewhere, an answer coalesced, an answer that might extricate him from this torture.

'The winner of the Grand National was ridden by a lady called Rachael Blackmore. Racheal is my Mum's middle name. And the 2,000 Guineas winner was the only horse on the bookmakers list that had odds of 25/1. My Mum was twenty-five when I was born.'

Freddie's embarrassment was completed when Linda turned to the camera in the studio and said in a sugary voice, 'Well, viewers, isn't that just *lovely*?'

Six

June 5ᵗʰ 2021

It was 4-25pm, five minutes before the Derby was due off, and Freddie was shaking his head. His mother, Amelia, and Jimmy were sitting on the sun-faded brown sofa in the lounge in front of their second-hand fifty-inch television which was far too big for such a small room, waiting in an intensely nervous state for the race to start.

'It won't win,' Freddie told them positively, 'Take a look at the price… it's 33/1.'

'Yeah, but it opened at 40/1,' Jimmy noted, 'Someone must fancy it.'

'Even so, there are eleven runners and there's a red-hot favourite and the experts have been saying it can't lose.'

'Don't you want it to win, Freddie?' piped up Amelia.

He paused for a second, 'Of course I do. All I'm saying is don't be too disappointed when Adayar trails in last… I was lucky to get two winners, three would be just crazy, especially when I know nothing about horses or betting.'

Mrs Wilson caught her son's eye and she gave him her 'don't worry son, it'll be okay' look. Freddie knew this slightly concerned, yet reassuring smile well enough by now. He'd been the recipient of the same smile after his Look North interview. His sister still thought his mum's middle name was Rachael, rather than Ruth, as Freddie hadn't had the heart to explain to her that he'd lied on live television.

In truth, Freddie had convinced himself Adayar wouldn't win. It would end the conversations about the Free Four-Timer that were the only topic of conversation among his friends, and still pervading the internet. The pressure would be off once the horse lost, and he and Jimmy could concentrate all their efforts on the prom in a few weeks' time.

The plans for the event were coming along nicely – Josh from Falstaff Bookmakers had been so pleased with the coverage they'd received, he'd offered to loan them a huge marquee for the event, and Jimmy had cajoled a local football club to gift them their spare pitch for the night, which was much better than the local park they'd originally chosen. They had a cracking DJ and bar staff booked, lots of lights, a generator, and Jimmy had somehow talked a local farmer into delivering a wagon-load of straw bales so they could create a bar and build makeshift tables and places to sit. In fact, he and Jimmy had thoroughly enjoyed pulling the prom together, despite the frustrations Covid had added to the arrangements. As the runners started to load into the starting stalls, Freddie reflected that it really wouldn't matter if Adayar lost. The 'Freddie Free Four-Timer' would be consigned to the news archives and forgotten about in a few weeks.

'Your horse is 25/1 now!' Jimmy reported.

'That means nothing. The horse doesn't know what price he is.'

Jimmy stared at his friend, 'I don't know how you can be so relaxed, there's half a million bleeding quid at stake here!'

Next to him on the sofa, Mrs Wilson made an audible gasping sound.

'Sorry about the language, Mrs W,' apologised Jimmy.

Smiling weakly, Mrs Wilson nodded, 'I didn't know it was that much money.'

'They've both got to win, Mum,' said Freddie, 'This one, and also it's got to snow on Christmas Day.'

'Still, it's nice to have that chance,' Mrs Wilson replied, her gaze never leaving the television screen as the commentator told the audience around the world that the race was off.

Just over two and a half minutes later, all four of them were dancing around in a tight circle, grasping each other's shoulders and whooping at the top of their voices. Adayar had not only won, he had won well, by a number of lengths. As their group hug broke up, gasping for breath, Mrs Wilson held up two flat hands and said, 'Hold on... Listen!'

Through the wall, they could hear their neighbour, Mr Faraday, screaming 'Yes, you beauty!' at the top of his voice. Out in the street, a cheer went up from across the road, then from a different direction, another whoop. There was soon a knock on the door, followed by several thumps when it wasn't immediately answered

When Freddie and Jimmy walked out of the front door and onto the pavement of their narrow little terrace, they were met by a knot of about twenty friends and neighbours. It was like there was a party going on. People they half-recognised ran forward to shake their hands. Mrs Wilson was hugged by several women, and one or two men too. Apparently Covid rules can be ignored when you'd chosen the 25/1 winner of the Derby, thought Freddie. Amelia was also unceremoniously hoisted onto the shoulders of a couple of teenagers who paraded the nine-year-old around the street between the parked cars.

'It looks like they've all backed Adayar,' their neighbour, Mr Faraday, told the two teenagers with a chuckle.

'I had... no idea,' Freddie replied, trying to take in the scene.

They watched as more people emerged from their houses to see what was going on and before long the entire street seemed to have spilled out onto the pavements and road. And then they spontaneously erupted into dancing once someone had cranked their CD player up to full volume and 'Summer Of Sixty Nine' by Bryan Adams began to be blasted down the street.

'I'll tell you something for nothing,' Mr Faraday added with a crackle of laughter, 'It better bloody snow at Christmas!'

Seven

June 14th 2021

'Trust Boris to cock it all up!'

Jimmy spat the words out with a viciousness that was quite out of character. He was standing, staring at his mobile phone in the middle of the football field that was due to be the site of their prom in only three days' time.

'It's a delay, that's all,' said Freddie without conviction.

'All that preparation, though…'

'I know. I know. We'll just have to get in touch with everyone and see whether we can push all the suppliers back a month.'

Jimmy eyed a wall of straw that had just been delivered.

'I somehow doubt that our friendly farmer will be too chuffed about loading eighty bales back onto his trailer, then bringing them back here in four weeks' time.'

Eight

July 19th 2021

Jimmy and Freddie watched the last few prom guests stumble somewhat drunkenly from the marquee, across the football pitch, and towards their waiting taxis. It was just after 3-00am and the two teenage organisers of the Year Thirteen Prom 2021 were sitting together on a bale of hay just outside the entrance to the marquee, their jackets folded on their knees, dicky-bows hanging raggedly around their necks, and their fancy white shirts unbuttoned. A string of battery powered fairy lights around the entrance were the only illuminations, as the generator had already left, as had the DJ. Once the last taxi pulled out of the football club car park, an eerie, but gratifying silence fell upon the football pitch.

'I'm shattered,' said Freddie, staring across the moonlit pitch trampled flat by prom-goers feet.

Jimmy thought for a moment, 'Me too. Shattered… but strangely satisfied.'

This brought a smile to Freddie's face. It had undoubtedly been a success. In fact, their prom qualified as a *big* success. It hadn't been a night without its little hiccups, but when all was said and done, they'd pulled it off. The two of them had actually pulled it off. With a budget of only £1,200, they'd given their year group a *proper* send-off.

'I saw you have a dance with Olivia,' Freddie ventured, 'Actually, didn't I see you with two or three different girls?'

Jimmy turned his head to grin at his friend, 'Yeah. I did dance with Olivia… and a few more too.'

'She didn't seem to be spending too much time with Steve?'

'No,' Freddie confirmed, his grin widening.

'Can I therefore assume…'

'You can!' Jimmy said with a chuckle, 'She broke up with Steve, so we had a dance.'

Jimmy's face suddenly became downcast and he looked away, 'To be honest, I found her a bit…'

'Boring?'

Jimmy smarted, 'No… well, yes. It was more that she was a bit self-obsessed. I can see why she got on with Steve, the two of them could talk endlessly about themselves and not actually listen to what each other was saying. I reckon Olivia only danced with me tonight because she thought I was important enough… mainly as I helped to organise the prom. Funny, isn't it. All the way through lockdown I was imagining what it would be like to be with her, and when I finally get to spend twenty minutes in her company she was a big disappointment.'

Freddie stuck out his bottom lip and nodded sagely in agreement, 'It's a shame, but not to worry, you weren't exactly short of dance partners.'

'Mmm. Funny that,' Jimmy mused, 'Actually, I got talking to one of Olivia's friends, Madison. She liked my short story – you know, the one you helped me practice for the talent night?'

'I remember.'

Freddie smiled inwardly. Jimmy certainly had a type. Madison was petite, but Rubenesque in proportions, and her dress had been eye-popping. However, at least this girl had a wicked sense of humour that might entertain Jimmy and give him a run for his money. Olivia had been good looking, but too one-dimensional for Jimmy.

'Yeah... I'm taking her out to the cinema next week.'

After a reflective pause, Jimmy asked, 'So what about you and Minnie? She looked incredible in that black outfit.'

Freddie crossed his arms, as if feeling a chill wind blow around him. He stood up and rubbed his hands up and down his sides.

'Yeah, Minnie looked... fantastic. Come on, we better get the marquee closed up and get a bit of kip. They'll be back in the morning for it, but I promised Josh we'd stay with it tonight so it doesn't get nicked.'

'Yeah, I know,' Jimmy replied, pushing himself up off the straw bale, 'Mind you, I don't know who would want a massive tent with the Falstaff Bookmakers logo splashed all over it!'

The two of them looked up at the gaudy yellow tent and Jimmy shook his head, 'It's a blummin' eyesore.'

'It did the job though,' Freddie said, a croaky tiredness suddenly apparent in his voice.

Something happened with that girl, Minnie, thought Jimmy. Freddie should be up a height after tonight. He'd been congratulated by virtually everyone - including the teachers that had turned up - for arranging and paying for everything. The night had been a triumph. Instead, he seemed downcast. Jimmy didn't know what had gone on, but Freddie would tell him eventually… he always did.

They spent twenty minutes cleaning up inside the marquee before bedding down in a pair of sleeping bags. Freddie had cut the twine on a couple of bales and they settled into the straw, soon accepting the sound of crunching straw that accompanied every movement.

'That Linda from Look North turning up with a film crew was unexpected,' said Jimmy, 'I thought you gave her a cracking interview. You're getting good at that stuff.'

Freddie smiled in the dark. He'd called the channel and reminded the producer, saying he'd give an interview and include a bit about his bet. In the event, he'd not had to talk too long about it, beyond saying he was hoping it would be a white Christmas. Still, it had been a bit of a coup that they turned up, and several of the guests had also got themselves on telly that night too. It had made the prom that little bit special.

'I just said what came into my head,' Freddie lied – he'd been rehearsing his short speech for days, 'But I was pleased with how the cameras made the entrance to the tent look like it was a red carpet premiere.'

Jimmy turned over and looked at his best friend in the dim light, making the straw crackle under his weight.

'Fred, did you enjoy it?' he asked

'Tonight you mean? Yeah, of course I did.'

'No, I mean the organisation of it all, pulling the event together from nothing?'

'I suppose so. But you did plenty too. All the arrangements for the guests, making sure everyone knew what to expect, and you got them all here. I couldn't have done it without you. Plus, you did all the announcements and thank-you's tonight. I couldn't have done that off the cuff like you can.'

'Well thanks, but did you get a kick from making it all happen, like I did?

'I don't know about a kick…'

Jimmy murmured a swearword under his breath, becoming irritated with the lack of a straight reply.

'Blimey Fred, just tell me… was it something you'd do again?'

Freddie contemplated for a few seconds, gazing up into the darkest corners of the tent, then closed his eyes.

'Yeah. I reckon I would,' he said with a yawn.

'So… neither of us have a wish to go to university,' Jimmy postulated, 'And we don't have a clue about what sort of job we want. But we both really enjoyed putting a complicated event together during Covid… I think we should do it again…'

'Tell you what, Jim,' Freddie said sleepily, 'If it's a white Christmas, we'll use the winnings to put on a party…'

Jimmy lay silent for a long moment, his eyes wide open, his mind racing. He saw far more possibility that just a party…

Presently he said, 'We could do all sorts… weddings, birthdays, corporate bashes, even rock concerts! I think we should do it even if you don't win that cash. We can call ourselves FredJim Events!'

Beside him, his best friend began to softly snore.

Nine

December 24th 2021

It was Friday night and it was cold. That was… *hopeful*, thought Freddie as he adjusted his hat and unfolded his collar to keep the icy breeze from making his neck go numb. His mother had been right, he should have worn a scarf, but it also meant there was an outside chance of snow. The weatherman had said it needed to drop by five degrees tonight to have a chance of being a white Christmas.

He'd been walking around this new-build estate for an

hour now, trying to work out what he would say, passing her house and telling himself he'd go ring the doorbell next time he completed another circuit. Now he was on her doorstep, fumbling with his gloves in order to push the doorbell.

Freddie never got to ring the bell, instead, a large middle-aged Jamaican man wearing a Santa hat flung the door open and frowned at him, but said nothing.

Eventually, the man asked in a West Indian accent, 'You going to sing, then?'

Freddie scrunched his face up in apology, 'I'm not a carol singer, I wondered if I could see Minnie?'

The man looked Freddie up and down, still holding the door open, and then called over his shoulder, 'Elizabeth! It's for you.'

There was the sound of squeaky floorboard footsteps coming down a flight of stairs, during which time the man maintained his wary gaze on the embarrassed looking lad on his doorstep. Freddie stood motionless, staring at his feet more than the man. He could have cheered when Minnie's face finally appeared behind her father.

Minnie registered shock at first. Most probably she'd been expecting a female friend, Freddie thought, rather than discovering a boy she hardly knew shivering on her doorstep. Her eyes popped a little as recognition registered. That was quickly followed by... was that embarrassment? She immediately shooed her father away and pulling a baggy cream cardigan around herself she stepped outside and clicked the door shut behind her.

'It's Freddie, isn't it?'

'Erm... yes.'

'Freddie Wilson, who prior to knocking on my door, stood on my feet at school, has ignored me on the talent nights, and then logged off before I could answer his question about my poem.'

He looked into her wonderfully dark eyes and was lost for a few seconds. When they narrowed and her brows dived

158

towards them, he found his voice.

'I'm sorry to call on Christmas Eve, Minnie, but I really needed to speak with you.'

He noticed she was already shivering, so quickly took a breath and soldiered on.

'I know this might sound… well, it will *sound* odd, but I wonder whether you would like to come for a walk with me?'

Her frown ironed out and she took on an amused expression. He'd take that, just at the minute. He'd been impressed she actually remembered him tripping over her feet all those months ago, before Covid.

'I'd like to explain something to you, and ummm… warn you to expect some attention if… something happens.'

'What on earth are you talking about?'

'If you could just come with me for a walk…'

'It's seven-o'clock on Christmas Eve, Freddie!' she exclaimed, casting her gaze furtively up and down her street to see if any of the neighbours were spying on her through their curtains.

Freddie's shoulders slumped. She was right. He'd judged it wrong. Yet both his mum and Jimmy had said he should try. She hardly knew him. He's been stupid to think she'd just fall into his arms and wander around the streets of Leeds on Christmas Eve with him. He'd been such an idiot at the prom too…

He looked up at her, her cheeks pinched red by the cold and opened his mouth to apologise and leave.

'Alright then!' she said abruptly before he could get anything out. She rolled her eyes at him, 'Hold on there a minute. I'll get a coat on, it's blummin' freezing out here.'

The door clicked shut and Freddie was left staring after her, his heart pounding.

A minute later, the door opened again. Minnie shouted something over her shoulder into the house about being back soon, and before he could say anything she was pushing him down her drive and out onto the pavement. He soon realised she was actually guiding him out of sight of her father, who was peering at the two of them with some consternation through a gap in the front room curtains. He was soon pulled away by a woman who grinned at the two of them momentarily before sliding the curtains shut.

'Was that your mum?'

'Yeah, she's cool, but my dad can be a bit… protective.'

'Mmm, I'm not the first lad to turn up on a cold winter's night to take you out for a walk?'

She drew to a halt, studying him with her head cocked to one side, as if trying to work him out.

'You're a proper funny onion, aren't you? I thought you were going to ask me to dance at the prom, but you just walked past me. You did it at least ten times! I started counting.

Freddie sheepishly inspected the pavement, his embarrassment at his inability to approach her had curled him up inside that night. So, instead, he'd kept busy, making sure everything ran smoothly. At least ten times eh? He was sure it had been less that that… but perhaps not.

Minnie took pity on the sorry soul in front of her and sucking in a deep breath, gave a long sigh, 'Isn't tomorrow an important day for you… if it snows you get a lot of money?'

He looked her up and down. She wore tight jeans, Doc Marten boots, a large black puffer jacket, and her father's Santa hat. She grinned at him, lighting up her round face with a crescent of white teeth.

'It's okay,' she told him, taking his arm and starting to walk, 'I'm drawn to weird, interesting people. So come on, Freddie, what's this all about. Did I leave something at the Prom you organised?'

Her ungloved hand felt warm against the inside of his bicep and he tried to forget she was so close to him. Freddie told himself to concentrate on what he had to say. What he had to tell her was important, and he had to say it right.

For the next forty minutes, they walked. Minnie proved

to be a good listener. She was also a kind listener. None of this came as a surprise to Freddie, he'd been getting to know her for the last two years, one stolen glance or overheard comment on zoom at a time, even though they'd hardly spoken. They passed houses with dozens of Christmas decorations, they passed plenty more with none. They agreed the ones with the old-fashioned trees in the windows were the best, although Minnie pointed out that bit of Christmas bling was still more than acceptable. Freddie found himself agreeing.

By the time they'd covered the first hundred yards, Freddie had admitted that he'd had a crush on her for the last eighteen months. Two streets later, he'd explained how he'd tried during all that time to pluck up the courage to speak with her.

By the time he'd explained about the free four-timer, they'd reached their destination.

From the top of Headingly Hill, Minnie took in the view of Leeds City centre. It was a blur of lights, creating a snow-globe of brightness in the distance.

'So, after I'd read my story at the talent night, you went online and chose three winners that were inspired… by me?'

Freddie smiled and shrugged. His embarrassment was gone though. She was still with him, they'd walked for two miles, and she was smiling.

'You chose the winner of the Grand National because Minella Times had a combination of my first and second name in the horse's name, Minnie and Ella,' she stated.

'Then you managed to find the winner of the 2,000 Guineas because you thought I had a flare for poetry… hence your choice of Poetic Flare.'

'Finally, you found the winner of the Derby this year because you'd seen from my Facebook page that my birthday is on January 25th. You then found there was only one horse on the ante-post list at that time who had odds of 25/1 – or 25th of the 1st – and Adayar was that horse.'

'And the bet will finish, one way or the other, tonight,' said Freddie, 'Just over there.'

'Hold on,' Minnie said, holding up a flat palm to him, 'I get that you decided to say it would snow on Christmas Day 2021 because I've let it be known that 'White Christmas' is my favourite Christmas song, but I don't understand... why would your bet finish in Leeds city centre? Surely it needs to snow in London for you to win?'

'There were odds for all the major cities in Great Britain. I chose for it to snow on the Leeds City Centre weather station at Leeds University,' Freddie replied, pointing to the illuminated School of Earth and Environment building.

Minnie slowly nodded, taking time to fully process this information. She continued to gaze out over the city centre as she spoke.

'And the reason you came to tell me this tonight, and drag me half the way across Leeds on Christmas Eve in the freezing cold, is because you wanted to warn me that if it does snow tonight, you intend to tell all the reporters, including the two million viewers on Look North, the *real* reason you managed to win over half a million pounds for free.'

She paused, and turned to fix her gaze on Freddie, holding him transfixed with her huge, beautiful hazel eyes, 'Not so you could ask me out?'

'I... I...' he flapped around, flabbergasted, trying to find words to express how he felt. Finally, he took a breath and trembling, took Minnie's hand in his.

'The only reason I'm here tonight is because of you. The only reason I might win half a million pounds is because of you. But I'd trade all of the money just to know that I'm not going to upset you, and we can still be, or even *become* friends.'

'Well...' she said, a sparkle of amusement entering her eye, 'You better ask me out quick.'

Freddie gulped. As he breathed out, his breath condensed. He watched the tiny cloud swirl around the two of them for a second before leaning forward and kissing Minnie on her cheek.

'When it comes to you, I'm not too good with words,' he said shyly.

She grinned and Freddie became momentarily fascinated as the moonlight sparkled in her eyes.

'Well, Mr Free Four-Timer Freddie,' she said, trying not to laugh at the tongue-twister, 'If it snows tonight, you have my permission to tell the media the true story of how you picked those winners.'

With that, she leaned forward and kissed him back on the lips.

Ten

December 25th 2021

The Leeds weather station based at Leeds University reported that at 3-55am on Christmas morning a light dusting of snow was detected. The only other snow that day was recorded in the Dales and in West Scotland. 2021 was officially registered as a 'White Christmas' in Great Britain.

'Doc' Jolley

TRANSCRIPT OF TAPED INTERVIEW WITH : Mr Samuel Maloney
DATE : 4th July 1979, 20:21
PRESENT: Mr Samuel Maloney, Detective Inspector Frank
Gould, Detective David Cauldercott.

DETECTIVE INSPECTOR GOULD : Okay, Mr Maloney. You claim to
have information which is pertinent to our inquiry. Please go
ahead.

MR SAMUEL MALONEY : Thank you, Detective Inspector. Might I
ask that I beg your patience, as it may seem some of what I'm
about to tell you is irrelevant, but be assured, it will prove
important to your inquiry.

DETECTIVE INSPECTOR GOULD : I will do my best. Please, continue.

MR SAMUEL MALONEY : I first met Wayne Jolley at Ripon races in
1975. He was in the racecourse stables, leaning against a box
wall. I noticed him because he was holding his head on one
side, watching the horses come and go. Wayne still does a lot
of that... watching horses with one eye almost closed and his
head tilted at forty-five degrees.
  He can't have been more than twenty-two. I'd have
been younger, probably seventeen, up from my base in the
south for one ride for my boss, and an apprentice jockey at the
time. I'd go anywhere in those days, desperate for rides, so I'd
made my first trip up to Ripon from Newmarket. To be
honest, despite my inexperience, I was too cocky and full of
myself, and Wayne took it upon himself to tell me so.
  In those days, the stable lads' canteen at Ripon was in
an old army hut, or at least, that's what it felt like, with
uniform bare wooden tables being housed in a prefabricated
shell with an asbestos sheet roof. It was dimly lit, had a
persistent draught, and was thoroughly depressing. So, when

I'd bought my lunch, I took my sandwich and one item of fruit outside and thought I'd go to find somewhere to eat it in the spring sunshine. It was a little after noon, and a couple of hours to the first race, so I had plenty of time before I needed to change into the silks for my one ride later in the afternoon. I'm a flat jockey you see.

I happened upon a sunny spot in a busy area of the stables, preferring to watch the world pass by, rather than eat completely on my own. Sitting with my back to a stable door, I set about my egg sandwich.

He was across the way, watching every horse as they came and went. Sometimes this tall, wiry figure would walk a few paces, with his head at that ridiculous angle. Once the horse had passed by, he'd return to his spot, near the door of one particular stable, and lean in exactly same place once more. It was so comical, I could hardly take my eyes from him. Backwards and forwards the young man went, a constantly quizzical frown upon his face, like that Patrick Moore chap, the astronomer. It was like he'd lost something and was checking that his possession wasn't attached to any of the passing horses.

Another peculiarity was that every single lad or lass that passed the intriguing young man called out a hello, or perhaps a short inquiry to his health or wellbeing. Some of them called him 'Doc'. He replied to them all, every single time including their names in his answer. I counted a Neil, Toby, Jane, Michael, Pat, and Rory in a matter of minutes.

The sandwich was awful, so I left it after only a bite or two, but managed to half finish my peach. Intrigued by the antics of the young chap, I ventured over. Before I was close enough to introduce myself and ask my burning question – what on earth was he doing? - he spoke to me.

'I'm Wayne Jolley. Peach stone,' he muttered without looking up. He followed a gelding's walk for a few paces before returning to his spot by the stable wall.

I must have looked confused, because he momentarily

flicked a questioning eye up at me. He repeated himself and pointed a finger over at the screwed up paper bag I'd left near a stable door, still holding the remains of my unfinished lunch.

'Peach stones kill horses,' he told me, scanning the walkway for the next horse, 'They eat the peach flesh but the stone gets stuck in their throats. They choke. You should pick it up.'

I took a moment to process this unexpected information, and like most people who meet Wayne for the first time, was uncertain how to respond. Despite his rather brusque advice, I found myself apologising.

'No need to apologise,' he said, still having not met my gaze, 'But best pick it up.'

I retrieved my discarded lunch and told Wayne, 'I'm Sam. So what are…'

'I know who you are,' he instantly interrupted, his eyes on the next horse walking between the lines of stables, 'You're Samuel Maloney. Apprentice jockey to Newmarket trainer, Vernon Lewis. Two wins from twenty-one rides and four places. You can do seven stone, twelve pounds. You ride Lily Hope today for your guv'nor. Nice young filly, but you got her unbalanced last time out at Newbury. You're too rough with her. You need to calm down and think about keeping her balanced on the undulating track here.'

Now I was closer to him, straight away I knew there was something different about him. Wayne's lazy eye, and the slight slackness around his jaw gave it away. Some people called it something different, something I'll not mention as I find the term distasteful, but I believe the medical people are giving it a proper name, they're saying Wayne has 'learning difficulties'. But you'd be wrong to say he was stupid, very wrong indeed.

'I didn't know I had a fan,' I replied, somewhat bewildered by his knowledge of my riding statistics and his bizarre analysis of my riding style, although I found it oddly impossible to take offence. I did wonder whether he'd just made the statistics up on the spot – I only kept count of my winners at the time – but the numbers did sound correct, 'And you've some strong views on my abilities as a jockey.'

'Oh, you'll do fine. Finesse is all you need Samuel Maloney, Bertolt Brecht said so.'

Wayne paused, tilting his head to the left, and peering skyward, then added, 'To live means to finesse the processes to which one is subjugated.'

'Bertolt Brecht eh?' I stated, still trying to size this chap up and frankly, at a loss for a suitable response.

He suddenly spun round, locked eyes with me for the first time, and smiled. It's the main thing I remembered about him that day. His smile. Despite the fact he had a pronounced forehead, and his eyes weren't quite aligned correctly, his face radiated incredible warmth. That's what a really genuine, truthful smile can do to you. It had a childlike innocence, and telegraphed a willingness to be open-minded without the need for words. I still think it's one of Wayne's greatest assets.

'I'm Wayne Jolley,' he told me, offering me his hand, 'Welcome to Ripon. It's your first time riding here, isn't it.'

It wasn't a question. He was telling me. I nodded.

I can't remember shaking his hand, but I must have done. A few minutes later I found myself alongside Wayne, leaning against the stable wall beside him and looking on as he assessed each horse as they passed. And strangely, I was chatting away. I should tell you now; Wayne makes friends. Lots of them. It's quite beguiling how he does it. I think it's because he manages to place people at their ease. He doesn't even have to say a great deal; he wasn't pumping me for information, yet he knew my life story within only a few minutes of meeting me. That's what tends to happen once you show interest, *real interest* in someone.

I eventually managed to ask, 'How about you? What's your story?'

He gave me a self-deprecating smile.

'Oh, everyone tells me I'm doing well. It seems to be a stock answer to someone like me.'

He must have read the confusion in my face, as he maintained eye contact for longer than was necessary, yet he offered nothing more.

'I've seen you watching the horses...'

Still no response, he was concentrating too hard on a young filly being led towards us.

At a loss to engage him and discover more about him, I became desperate.

'Is there someone here, you know... looking after you?'

Hearing those demeaning words again makes me cringe. When I remember them now, I wish I could rub them out; somehow delete them from our first conversation. Wayne must have heard something similar so many times, perhaps in different words, yet the subtext is always the same; you're different, and without saying it directly, I'm assuming you don't belong here, at least not on your own, not someone *like you*.

However, he smiled again.

'I'm working,' he said levelly, his eyes swivelling, caught by the filly taking a turn and walking back past him. The lad leading up called a greeting to Wayne as they passed. He replied, using the lad's name in his reply.

'Doing what work, exactly?' I pressed, keen to move on and grateful he hadn't taken offence at my previous question.

Before I received an answer, a short, dark skinned man called out from further down the line of stables. His jet black hair was plastered to his skull and I instantly recognised him as George Manning, a trainer of some note in the north, and as I had already discovered, Wayne's employer.

'Jolley!' George cried once more hoisting an arm and waving it in a follow me motion, 'Ha'way lad.'

Wayne told me he had better go, smiled for the last time, and hurried off. I watched him go. For a tall man, he had a quick walk. Rather than stride along as one would expect, the young man appeared to have springs in his knees and skipped along at a canter, his arms held awkwardly straight. I remember it put me in mind of John Cleese.

The stable lad who had called out to Wayne passed by me again and I fell into stride with him, determined to discover more about the man with whom I'd enjoyed one of the strangest encounters of my life.

'That's Doc Jolley,' the lad told me in answer to my query, 'He's a fixer.'

'Fixer?'

'Yeah. He's not a real sawbones. Just called that 'cos of what he does. He fixes the horses.'

I drilled him for more information.

'He sort of talks to 'em. Y'know, the daft, naughty, or downright violent ones. Some say he whispers to 'em. Whatever the Doc does, it works. He gets them eatin' out of his 'ands and better than that, he can tell what's up with 'em.'

I know I'm being a bit theatrical, doing the voices and telling my story like a tu'penny thriller. I guess it's my upbringing, my Mother was an actress. But it's important you understand the world according to Wayne Jolly.

The second time I met Wayne was five weeks later. We spent five hours together in the casualty department of Redcar Hospital; he got a warm bed for the night and I was forced to sleep in a cold Ford Cortina. I take huge pleasure in remembering that evening. That's because I was instrumental in introducing Wayne to Charity, his wife.

I wasn't even aware he'd been at the races until late in the afternoon. As I walked, saddle over my arm, back to the weighing room having finished mid-division in a lowly rated handicap, I spotted Wayne standing beside the parade ring, his head buried in a copy of The Sporting Life.

'You were right,' I called to him as I approached.

He put his head jerkily on one side and glanced up over his paper, smiling that transparently genuine smile at me once more, and I couldn't help but smile back. I challenge anyone who receives that smile from Wayne not to.

'Hello, Samuel,' he responded, informing a total stranger next to him, 'That's my friend, Samuel.'

The chap gave Wayne that look. The one that is amiable enough, but is also carefully assessing whether this complete stranger is right in the head.

'I didn't have chance to thank you. That filly, Lily Hope… I won on her at Ripon after taking your advice.'

'Softer hands,' he said, slowly nodding, 'It made her trust you.'

'Yes,' I agreed with a chuckle, 'Say, how about us meeting up after the last race? I'd love to know more about your, erm… fixing thing.'

I left Wayne blinking down at his newspaper, with an agreement to meet at the racecourse gates after I'd weighed in following the last race.

A second placing, followed by a Stewards' Enquiry meant I was late. When I got to the racecourse gates it was well after five o'clock, the Tattersalls area of the course was deserted, and there was no sign of Wayne. That was, until I went into the car park. I heard scuffling and a kerfuffle kicked off to my left. Two youths, fuelled by alcohol, discontent, and no doubt, ignorance, were thrashing someone with their knee length lace-up boots. It took me a only a moment to recognise the poor devil receiving the kicking.

I may not be statuesque, or endowed with generous proportions, but even at the age of seventeen, years of work riding had made me tough and given me steel-like muscles. I ran headlong into the first of Wayne's attackers, beating him back with flailing fists. While he lay on the tarmac, winded, and nursing a bloody nose, I set about the other. He soon backed away, more out of shock than any injury I managed to bestow upon him. The second young man helped his pal up from the ground and they shambled away, shouting obscenities over their shoulders as they went.

Wayne was in a bad way. Crouched in a trembling ball,

hands over his head, he wouldn't respond to anything I said. He was in shock, and it took me the best part of five minutes to get him to his feet.

I eventually managed to bundle the frightened, tear-stained twenty-two year old into my second hand Ford Cortina and forty minutes later he was lying on a bed in the local hospital being pored over by two fresh-faced doctors. A lost tooth lay in a metal dish by the bed, along with a heap of bloodied swabs, but it was soon established that although Wayne was badly bruised around his ribs, and had sustained several cuts to his face and hands, the only thing broken was his nose, the evidence of which Wayne shows off proudly to this day. I believe his bent nose evens his face up, a fact I remind him of whenever the opportunity arises.

It took almost two hours from the moment I broke the fight up, to when Wayne emerged from his shock and started to speak and smile again. That's something you should remember, as I believe it's relevant to his current situation.

I spent the entire evening in Redcar Hospital at his bedside as he received the attention of various doctors, nurses, and ancillary staff. It was an education. I was able to watch Wayne at close quarters as he worked his magic on all of those around him. He soon had the entire ward wrapped around his little finger, and the wonderful thing about it was… he had no idea he was doing it.

I know he'll forgive me for telling you that he was in sparkling form that evening. Once the shock of being victimised had receded, I took the opportunity to pump him for information during the quieter moments.

Wayne had no living family. When his mother died, he left his hometown of Hull at the age of nineteen, and unable to drive, he thumbed his way over the Wolds to Malton. He found his way to Norton, and Langton Road where he systematically visited every training yard he came across, offering his services as a dab hand with a brush and shovel. I've no doubt his demeanour was the reason he was turned away from the first two, but the third yard was more enlightened and offered him a job and lodging.

The George Manning yard became Wayne's new home. I once asked him what drove him to leave Hull to work around horses and to my considerable consternation he replied, 'Donkeys,' presuming further explanation wasn't required. I eventually managed to extract the full story from him.

Before his mother became too ill to work, she ran a string of donkeys on the east coast, spending the summer months ferrying them to whichever beach she believed would be the most lucrative in order to offer holidaymakers rides along the sands. He grew up with donkeys, learned to feed them, care for their mishaps, births, and deaths, and most importantly… he watched them. Alone in a windswept paddock close to the North Sea coast, Wayne felt the first twinges of what would become his chosen profession. With his mother becoming increasingly immobile and Wayne unable to manage the business, the donkeys had to be sold, and there was nothing to keep him in Hull once she died.

I need to back track here. I've told you some of Wayne's abilities, I should probably touch upon one or two of the things he finds difficult. For one, he struggles with understanding anything with a double meaning. Sarcasm, or pretty much anything stated with a subtext is lost on him. He's a voracious reader, but can't write. He's an accomplished artist, but signs, such as road signs without words, can stump him. That's how he met his wife at the hospital.

Wayne had recovered enough to shuffle off to the toilet and I had my head in his racing paper when a small, neat nurse with deep brown hair piled onto her head in a bun pulled the curtain back a little in his little semi-private bed in the hospital.

'Are you Samuel?' she asked brightly.

When I indicated I was, she swept the curtain back to reveal a rather confused looking Wayne standing with her.

'We bumped into each other in the corridor,' the nurse explained as she helped him onto the bed, 'I caught him just before he accidentally entered the nurses changing room.'

'I got the signs jumbled up,' Wayne agreed, barely able to take his eyes off the girl in her mid-twenties. The nurse's cheeks flared red for a moment and I immediately sensed Wayne had already managed to work some of his magic on her. Studying his face again, I understood that I 'd mistaken his confused look. He was in fact ogling the poor girl.

'This is Charity, she's a friend,' Wayne said, still unable to wrench his gaze from her, 'This is my friend, Samuel.'

'Just Sam will do,' I told Charity.

Wayne glanced at me, a frown forming.

'You prefer Sam?'

I gave a little shrug. I'd never been that bothered by either, but my mother had always called me Samuel.

'No, that's wrong,' he insisted, shaking his head, 'I shall still call you Samuel. That's your name in the race listings, that's what I shall call you.'

'Is he always this forthright?' Charity asked me, clearly amused by the two of us, busying herself by setting things right around the bed. She bit her bottom lip as she worked, glancing up at her patient from time to time. Wayne never took his eyes off Charity for the next three hours. Whenever she walked past or checked on him, Wayne would tilt his head in the same way he did when watching a horse, but significantly, his eyes were much softer.

At just after eleven in the evening, a junior doctor appeared and after a final cursory check, told us with bad bruising and more than likely, a couple of cracked ribs, it would be best if Wayne stayed in overnight. Wayne didn't complain, in fact, he accepted the news with childlike glee.

I spent a cold and uncomfortable night sleeping in my car, and the next time I saw Wayne was after breakfast the next morning. He'd made it down to the hospital canteen and greeted me with a huge grin.

'Samuel! I've asked her to marry me!' he announced before I'd had time to sit down.

'Charity, the nurse. I've asked her.'

'And she's said yes?' I boggled.

'No, of course not,' he said with a smile, 'But I'm having breakfast with her!'

Charity arrived at the table a few minutes later. Now off-duty, she wore jeans, t-shirt, and baseball boots, and with her hair let down, her locks spiralled around her shoulders and framed a pretty round face. I couldn't help noticing that her progress across the cafeteria was tracked, and I daresay enjoyed by several of the younger male patients taking breakfast. I didn't quite know what to expect, but, by the time I'd helped Wayne into my car forty-five minutes later, I was certain that Charity was perfect for him. Wayne had seen it within the first few minutes of meeting her last night. It had simply taken a dullard like me a lot longer.

I drove Wayne back to Malton and dropped him at George Manning's yard, promising to call him the next time I was in Yorkshire.

Three weeks later, I was summoned into the yard office of my boss in Newmarket and told I must return a telephone call. The boss insisted I did it straight away, as the idiot boy calling me had done so fifteen times in the last hour and he was getting sick of telling him I was still out riding the second lot.

Wayne must have been sat over the phone, waiting for it to ring. He was almost breathless with excitement and shouted out to me before I had chance to say more than one word.

'She's said yes!'

Wayne bellowed this in triumph, then added, 'And I only had to ask seven times before she agreed, Samuel!'

The one thing about Wayne; he's relentless. When he gets something into his head, he will persevere.

Well, that's about it, Detective Inspector. If you

interview Wayne again, please, please bear in mind what I've told you.

DETECTIVE INSPECTOR GOULD : Thank you for coming in Mr Maloney. Mr Jolley has still said nothing to us apart from one thing. He keeps repeating that he killed Mr George Manning.

Tell me, would you say Mr Jolley is capable of violence when he doesn't get his way?

MR SAMUEL MALONEY : Absolutely not. Wayne isn't capable of any sort of aggression. If you'd seen him work with horses, you'd know that whilst he can be relentless, he is also relentlessly patient.

I watched Wayne work for the first time in the autumn of 1975. I can sum the experience up in a single word: revelatory.

Once married, he and Charity had initially rented a flat in Malton, but for reasons that were unknown to me at the time, he had left his employment at the yard in Norton and they had chosen a small terraced house in York, close to the County Hospital where Charity now worked.

It transpired that Manning, the trainer Wayne had been working for, had been charging owners, and even other trainers for Wayne's services. Charity discovered that due to Wayne's extraordinary success at taming the wilder racehorses, and his unearthly ability to locate niggling physical problems in horses that could make the difference between winning and losing races, the trainer was charging rather a lot of money. None of this money was reflected in Wayne's pay packet, which was still that of a non-riding stable lad. Wayne was reluctant to leave his job at first, because he owed Manning plenty for taking him in and giving him a home when others turned him away. Manning was also the one who recognised his gift with racehorses, and allowed him to develop his skills. But Charity took him in hand and gave him the confidence to quit his job in Malton.

If you remember, I told you that Wayne isn't great with numbers and writing. However, with Charity by his side, who it turned out was not only a loving wife, but a very savvy businesswoman, Wayne was able to set up as a freelance horse fixer. Very soon, he was known all over Yorkshire, and with my help over the next few years, he was introduced to a whole new set of customers in Newmarket.

I was happy to recommend him, because what he was doing with horses was incredible.

I drove him to a training yard in Middleham, North Yorkshire in January 1976 during the off-season. It was a large yard, more than a hundred horses there, run by a chap called Arthur Field. He had an expensive colt who was simply refusing to be broken. It took three stable lads to lead this hulking great colt, kicking and bucking, out of a stable and into a fenced menage.

'No one can get close to him,' Arthur told us, 'He's mental, and downright dangerous. Our vet can't get anywhere near him. He's already given one of my lads a nasty kick that had him in bed for three days. If you can't sort him out, he'll have to be put down. This is his last chance.'

It took Wayne forty minutes. By the time he'd finished there were twenty lads, lasses, and work riders watching him work with this colt. They were even being called from the training yard next door. It was jaw-dropping. Wayne has this… way about him. A calm, confident, careful way about him when he's with a horse. He almost becomes a horse, a companion to them, and he speaks their language… a silent, yet compelling language of movement that imparts trust into his equine patients. It was nothing short of spellbinding. By the end of his time in that menage, Wayne was able to run his hands all over the colt, who stood mute and motionless, completely relaxed. With no collar or rein, the colt then followed him around the menage, keeping a single pace behind him. It earned him a round of applause from the crowd, who all knew the colt was the most difficult horse in the yard.

'He had a thoracic vertebrae out of place, just below his withers. I imagine every time someone has tried to lie over him during the breaking process, he's been in excruciating pain,' Wayne reported to the trainer, 'I've manipulated it back into place, but it's been out for so long, you need to keep an eye on him for a few days and let it settle. He's not a bad horse, he's just been protecting himself. If he shows any sort of attitude again, get someone to look at his fourth thoracic.'

Word of mouth is the way business is done in the racing industry, and Wayne's services were soon in high demand, and they have been ever since. Doc Jolley is who you call in when you have a horse that needs fixing. Which brings me to the reason I've given you this potted history of my relationship with him and the man he is… because despite the evidence, there is no way Wayne Jolley could have murdered his ex-employer.

DETECTIVE INSPECTOR GOULD: Mr Jolley has already confessed several times to the killing. It's the only thing he has said, and is quite certain.

MR SAMUEL MALONEY: I understand that. But he will be in shock. He becomes monosyllabic when he's had a shock, just like the time he was attacked at Redcar races. Besides, Wayne always states everything as he sees it. He tells the truth, whether it's black or white, and he only answers what he's asked. Most importantly, he sometimes fails to understand the nuance of certain situations and statements.

DETECTIVE INSPECTOR GOULD : I'm sure that's true; however Mr Jolley has stated he killed Mr Manning. Mr Jolley left Mr Manning in the stable, went to the tack room and found a sharp knife and returned to the stable where he stabbed a defenceless old man. He's admitted this, several times. He was found at the bottom of Mr Manning's stables in Malton with the knife still in his hands, and covered in Mr Manning's blood.

And with your information regarding Mr Manning, we now have a strong motive. Mr Jolley was plainly seeking revenge for being manipulated by his ex-employer. For a number of years he wasn't receiving due payment while his employer earned huge sums off the back of his work. We have a witness who reported Mr Jolley demanding money prior to the killing of Mr Manning.

I can confirm that your friend has been arrested and whilst I thank you for coming forward to provide your testimony, your friend will be charged with murder. He has confessed, and I've no doubt he will be held on remand until his trial.

MR SAMUEL MALONEY: Did you know that Wayne has what they call an *eidetic memory*? It's sometimes referred to as a photographic memory, although that's a poor description, as the range of detail he is capable of recalling is incomparable.

I can tell by your reaction that you didn't know.

Ask him. Just… ask him. Ask Wayne to recount everything from the moment he met Manning earlier today to when your policeman arrived. Then you'll know for certain whether he murdered George Manning.

END OF INTERVIEW: 21:27pm

TRANSCRIPT OF TAPED INTERVIEW WITH : Mr Wayne Jolley
DATE : 4 July 1979, 22:03pm
PRESENT: Detective Inspector Frank Gould, Detective David Cauldercott, Mr Wayne Jolley.

DETECTIVE INSPECTOR GOULD : Okay, Mr Jolley. I've spoken with your friend Mr Maloney. Against my better judgement, I'm giving you a last chance to recount what happened at the stables of Mr George Manning earlier today, before I charge you.

MR WAYNE JOLLEY: I killed the Guv'nor, I mean Mr George Manning… How is Samuel? Is Charity here? Please tell them not to worry.

DETECTIVE INSPECTOR GOULD: Mr Maloney is fine, Wayne. Your wife is with him, and they are waiting downstairs. Mr Maloney seems to think you didn't kill Mr Manning, despite what you keep telling us. He also claims you have a photographic memory. Is that true Wayne?

MR WAYNE JOLLEY: When can I go home? I'd like to see my wife and my friend, Samuel. Can I see them Detective Gould?

DETECTIVE INSPECTOR GOULD: You need to answer my questions, Wayne. If you answer my questions truthfully, I'll see about letting your wife visit you. Can you answer my questions, Wayne?

For the tape, Mr Jolley has shut his eyes and started to hum…

MR WAYNE JOLLEY: Yes Detective Gould. I have an eidetic memory. Can I see my wife and Samuel now? I did answer your question.

DETECTIVE INSPECTOR GOULD: That's good Wayne, but I have more questions. Let's start at the beginning. I need you to tell me everything from when you arrived at Mr Manning's yard earlier today. Can you do that for me?

MR WAYNE JOLLEY: Certainly Detective Gould. Ten fifty-five; I parked my new car in Mr Manning's car park at March Hare Stables. I've just passed my driving test. It's a Vauxhall Viva, registration number P56…

DETECTIVE INSPECTOR GOULD : You don't need to give us that level of detail, just tell me what happened.

MR WAYNE JOLLEY : You asked me to tell you *everything*. You said, I need you to tell me everything from…

DETECTIVE INSPECTOR GOULD : Tell me *everything you did*, Wayne. Not literally everything.

For the tape, Mr Jolley is nodding.

MR WAYNE JOLLEY : The Guv'nor, that's Mr Manning, came out to meet me from the second barn. The Guv'nor said hello and it was good to see me, and we shook hands. We went down to the small paddock with the two big oak trees in it and I looked at a gelding. Once it had walked and I'd touched it, I told the Guv'nor it had a kissing spine. The Guv'nor wasn't happy with that and said some things and swore.

DETECTIVE INSPECTOR GOULD : He was angry with you?

MR WAYNE JOLLEY : No, he was disappointed. It was a good horse, worth a lot of money, and the kissing spine meant the gelding wouldn't be able to race again. The Guv'nor said, 'The owner ain't goin' to be happy, that's for sure,' and then he swore quite a bit.

Do you want me to tell you the swear words?

DETECTIVE INSPECTOR GOULD : No, that's okay Wayne. Please continue. What happened next?

MR WAYNE JOLLEY : The Guv'nor said he had another horse. An unbroken three-year-old colt in the isolation stables at the bottom of the yard. It had arrived in the yard a week ago, but was now refusing to leave its box and was being naughty. The Guv'nor asked me to take a look and see what I thought.

We walked together to the small isolation barn and the Guv'nor said he was sorry about how things had ended between us. I told him Charity wasn't sure I should be helping him anymore. But I told the Guv'nor I was happy to do it because he'd given me my chance and looked after me for two years. He said I was a good kid and it sounded like my wife had her head screwed on right.

DETECTIVE INSPECTOR GOULD : So you didn't argue about money?

MR WAYNE JOLLEY : No, not until we walked into the barn and got inside the colt's stable.

DETECTIVE INSPECTOR GOULD : This is important, Wayne. Why were you arguing about money?

MR WAYNE JOLLEY : The Guv'nor asked me to look at the colt. It was a big horse, timid, and frightened. I told the Guv'nor the colt hadn't been handled right and he said it was a homebred and had been out in the field with its mother for the last year and probably hadn't had much, if any contact with people.

I found a problem with the colt's near-rear foot. The colt was in pain from an abscess that was deep in his foot. It was invisible, but the colt allowed me to touch it after I'd spent fifteen minutes with him and won his confidence. I told the Guv'nor that was why he was playing up and wouldn't leave his stable. Once he walked on the concrete floor in the barn it would be painful.

The Guv'nor told me to go get a paring knife from the tack room so we could see whether we could prick the abscess. So I went up the yard and returned with the paring knife. And after I'd cleaned the hoof we argued about Monet.

DETECTIVE INSPECTOR GOULD : Wayne, think carefully. What did you and Mr Manning argue about?

MR WAYNE JOLLEY : Monet, the colt. We argued about Monet.
The Guv'nor wanted to dig into his foot to release the pressure, but I told him the abscess was too deep and I didn't think the colt would stand for his foot being pierced. I said we should give the abscess a few more days to either crack his hoof and come out naturally, or wait until the vet could sedate him and even block the nerves to his foot so the colt didn't get upset. The Guv'nor raised his voice and told me this was Monet, the first offspring by Rubens, and the owner wanted to see him broken in a week's time and if Monet wasn't fixed, he couldn't break him in. I told the Guv'nor he should wait until Monet was ready to accept people being around him. The conversation became... heated.

DETECTIVE INSPECTOR GOULD : Just a minute Wayne... What was the colt's name?

MR WAYNE JOLLEY : Monet. Like the painter. What's the matter Detective Gould, why are you frowning like that?

DETECTIVE INSPECTOR GOULD : Don't worry about me, Wayne. Okay. What happened next?

- TWENTY SECONDS OF SILENCE -

...for the tape, Mr Jolley has become emotional and has tears in his eyes. I have handed Mr Jolley my handkerchief.

MR WAYNE JOLLEY : Monet was starting to get agitated. The Guv'nor said he couldn't wait for a vet, and took the paring knife from me. He took hold of the colt's foot between his legs, with his back to Monet and started to scrape at the sole of the foot with the knife pointed towards himself, looking for where the abscess might be. I warned the Guv'nor that he should stop, but he didn't...

Monet squealed and kicked the Guv'nor forwards and across the stable. He landed on his stomach, hitting the brick base of the stable hard, and made a gurgling sound. I rushed to the Guv'nor's side and rolled him over...

- FIFTEEN SECONDS OF SILENCE -

The Guv'nor had landed on the paring knife and it had gone deep into his chest. He was groaning, and his hands were on the handle of the knife. When I rolled him over, the blade was still in him, but the Guv'nor pulled it out, even though I immediately told him not to. I'd killed him... If I hadn't rolled him over, he'd have still got the knife in him and his lungs wouldn't have filled with blood and...

DETECTIVE INSPECTOR GOULD : They call your Doc Jolley don't they, Wayne?

MR WAYNE JOLLEY : Yes. They do.

DETECTIVE INSPECTOR GOULD : So you know about medical stuff do you?

MR WAYNE JOLLEY : I've inspected lots of dead horses and taken them apart to understand how they tick. I've also read dozens of medical books, both for horses and humans. It helps to understand the anatomy of both.

DETECTIVE INSPECTOR GOULD : If the blade of the knife has stayed in his chest, would Mr Manning have lived?

MR WAYNE JOLLEY : Leaving it in would have given him a chance. Instead, he died quickly. The blade would have held the walls of the lungs together and stopped the blood. But by rolling him over, I…

DETECTIVE INSPECTOR GOULD : Our mortician says the knife caught the edge of Mr Manning's heart as well as his lungs, Wayne. Roll him over or leave him face down, either way your Guv'nor would have gone quickly. At least he died with someone who cared about him looking into his eyes. Did he say anything?

MR WAYNE JOLLEY : The Guv'nor said, 'Should have listened to you Doc. Stay an innocent. You're a one-off,' and then he died…. Why are you smiling, Inspector?

DETECTIVE INSPECTOR GOULD : Your Guv'nor was right. You should stay the way you are, Wayne. Don't let anyone change you.

You'll need to sign a few things for me, but it's time for you to go now. Your wife and your friend, Samuel, are waiting for you downstairs. Follow me Wayne, I'll see you out.

END OF INTERVIEW: 22:37pm

Enjoyed these stories?

I do hope you have enjoyed reading these horseracing and betting stories. If you have, I'd *really* appreciate it if you would visit the Amazon website and leave a rating and perhaps a short review. Your ratings and reviews help readers find my books, which in turn means I can dedicate more time to writing.

Simply visit **www.amazon.co.uk** and search for 'Richard Laws'.

You can also register for my book alert emails and news on upcoming books at **www.thesyndicatemanager.co.uk**

Many thanks,

Richard Laws
May 2022

Printed in Great Britain
by Amazon

81829353R00109